Just One Night

The Kingston Family
Book 1

NEW YORK TIMES BESTSELLING AUTHOR
Carly Phillips

JUST ONE NIGHT

She's the woman he can't live without.
The one he can't risk screwing up their relationship by sleeping with her.

Linc Kingston doesn't accept anything less than perfection. Not in his billion-dollar business or in his personal life. He has it all. Except one thing. His personal assistant and best friend in his bed, moaning his name. No matter how much Linc wants her, she's completely off-limits.

Jordan Greene grew up the daughter of the housekeeper at the Kingston estate, where she met and bonded with Linc at a young age, despite their economic differences. But no matter how close they are now or how much their attraction simmers beneath the surface, they're still from two different worlds. Besides, Jordan isn't about to risk losing her best friend for one sensual night.

Jordan might be the only woman who can handle Linc and his domineering, bossy attitude, but beneath that gruff exterior is a vulnerable man who, despite his wealth, has had a less-than-charmed life. And when Linc's father dies, she's there for him—unwavering in her friendship.

Until one night of passion and a positive pregnancy test changes everything.

Chapter One

LINC KINGSTON'S FATHER was a pompous jerk, a philandering womanizer, an asshole of the first order, and he was dead, leaving behind four legitimate children and one illegitimate daughter. That they knew of.

Linc spread the canceled checks he'd found weeks ago across his desk. As he'd discovered yesterday from the private investigator he'd hired, the trail had led to a sister he knew nothing about, and the information had sent him reeling. Who knew what other surprises awaited in the wake of Kenneth Kingston's death of a heart attack a month earlier?

Picking up a glass of Macallan 18, not his first or even his second, he finished the contents. Without hesitation, he poured himself another with the bottle he'd taken from the bar in the corner of the office that had once been his father's.

"Slow down or you'll end up sleeping here tonight," his brother Xander said. Feet kicked out in front of him, he leaned back in his chair.

"I have a car waiting to take me home. I can get as

drunk as I want." Linc lifted the tumbler to his lips.

Xander groaned. "Look, I get it. I'm not happy about the news either, but it's not like we thought Dad was a stellar human being. Are you really shocked he knocked up his secretary nineteen years ago and left a daughter to show for it?"

"No." Linc took another sip. "But I am horrified by the fact that at some point he looked up the kid's mother, found out the child was in foster care, and left her there." Linc's private investigator had tracked down Tiffany Michaels and gotten the story. Linc's stomach churned at how his sister had been treated by both of her parents.

Xander glanced up at the ceiling, adjusting his black-framed eyeglasses he wore after a long day staring at a computer screen. "I changed my mind. I could use a drink myself."

With a shake of his head, Xander rose, walked to the bar, grabbed a tumbler, and brought it back to the desk. He picked up the bottle, poured himself a drink, and settled into his chair before indulging in a hefty gulp.

"What do Dash and Chloe say?" Xander asked of their siblings.

Of course Xander wouldn't know how they'd taken the news. While Linc was dealing with their late father's estate, the business he'd been helping to run for years, and the paperwork after their father's death, Xander had been closed up in his home office writing. He was a marine turned thriller writer after his return stateside whose books had been made into blockbuster movies, and he often got lost in his own world. Linc had called him here tonight to fill him in about their sister.

He glanced at the surprise checks he'd found. Everything relating to the family real estate business banking was online. That Kenneth had obviously opened an account to hide these payments spoke volumes about what their father was capable of when it came to his penchant for deception.

"I dragged his ass out of the studio to talk to him. Did it on the phone because, as you know, he's holed up and working with the band. He listened, said it figured Dad would leave us with this kind of surprise, and went back to work."

Dash was the lead singer of The Original Kings, a rock band he'd been a part of since he was in high school. After years of playing bars and smaller gigs, they'd been discovered, and their success was massive and worldwide. When home in New York, Dash had a house near Xander's in the Hamptons fully equipped with a studio and enough room for his bandmates to crash.

Linc rubbed the back of his stiff neck with his

fingers.

Xander nodded. "Dash is focused when he's working."

"Sound familiar?" Linc asked wryly. "Anyway, he texted me later and said he wanted to meet her, so he's fine. Mellow and typical Dash."

"And Chloe?" Xander drummed his fingers on the arm of his chair.

"She's upset. Devastated she had a sister she never knew about and one who obviously grew up in way different circumstances than us." It turned Linc's stomach. He didn't have details of this sibling's upbringing, but he knew it wouldn't be pretty. "Aurora," he said.

"What?" Xander asked.

"Our sister's name is Aurora. I think we should start getting used to it."

A knock sounded on his door, and his personal assistant and best friend, Jordan Greene, walked inside, her dark hair pulled back in a sleek ponytail, her black slacks and silk blouse as immaculate as they'd been this morning. After her upbringing, Jordan prided herself on being able to afford quality clothing and looking her best. No more hand-me-downs from her sister.

"I'm leaving for the night. Anything I can get you before I go?" she asked, as she did every night he stayed later than her. They both worked long hours.

Xander turned to face her. "Hey, Jordan. You weren't at your desk when I came in. I almost thought you gave up on dealing with my brother." He jerked a finger back at Linc and laughed.

"Shut up, asshole." Linc scowled at his sibling.

Jordan chuckled. "We all know I'm the only one who will put up with him. I can't subject my fellow females to his bossy personality at work."

"I am not that bad," Linc muttered.

"Yes, you are," they both said at the same time, and their joint laughter echoed around the room.

Linc shook his head as they made fun of him. It wasn't unusual for Jordan to gang up on him with one of his siblings, and maybe he deserved it. He wasn't always easy.

Jordan's mother, Tamara, had been the Kingston's housekeeper throughout their childhood. As a result, Jordan knew all of his siblings well but mostly Linc as they'd bonded early on. They'd become not just best friends but a united duo. Despite their different backgrounds, they'd clicked. After school she'd come to their house to do her homework while waiting for her mother to finish working, and Linc used to join her.

Getting her to become his assistant after he'd graduated business school had been the smartest thing he'd ever done. His schedule was always up-to-date, she knew what he wanted almost before he asked, and their friendship had only deepened.

He met her blue-eyed stare. "I'm good. You can take off for the night."

"Awesome. I'm going to pick up sushi for dinner on my way home. See you in the morning!" she said, bright and cheery as always. "Night, Xander."

"Good night, Jordan." Xander gave her a wave before turning back to face Linc, a curious expression on his face as the door clicked shut behind her.

"What?" Linc all but barked the question at his brother, who still stared at him as if he had something to say.

"Have you really not fucked her yet?" Xander asked.

"You asshole. Don't talk about Jordan like that."

Xander's grin told Linc he'd nailed him, prodding him on purpose to get a reaction, and Linc had given the bastard what he wanted.

"Come on, seriously. Why haven't you two gotten together?" Xander finished his drink and put the glass down on the old mahogany desk.

"Want more?" Linc lifted the bottle of scotch.

Xander shook his head. "No, but I do want an answer."

Knowing he needed more alcohol for this, Linc

poured himself another drink. He was getting wasted far deeper and faster than he preferred, liking to keep his wits about him. But after hearing about his new sister and processing how she'd been raised when a family with money would have welcomed her, he needed to numb his feelings.

"Linc!" Xander kicked the desk with his foot. "Where did you go?"

He blinked and looked into his empty glass. "Sorry. What did you want to know?" The alcohol was getting to him.

"I asked why you and Jordan haven't hooked up."

"Because she's my best friend, and I couldn't live without her if things didn't work out." Even if she had a body his fingers itched to touch, lips he was dying to kiss, and sky-blue eyes that could see into his soul, he had to keep his hands … and mouth to himself. Over the years, the restraint had cost him, but he'd managed not to step over that line.

He'd grown up well aware of his father's indiscretions, mostly with the women who worked for him, and Linc had gone out of his way not to be anything like the man. If he was more serious, asked more of others, then so be it. As long as he wasn't leaving work to meet up with a mistress or sleeping with one of his assistants or secretaries, Linc could look himself in the mirror each day.

Xander tipped his head to one side. "Makes sense, I guess."

Xander knew all about heartbreak after being duped by a young, hot Hollywood actress he'd fallen in love with while in LA during the filming of his first book made into a movie. He wouldn't argue with Linc's explanation about why he kept things platonic with Jordan. Not when it meant avoiding both heartbreak and the potential ending of an important friendship.

"You ever wonder if she would want more?" Xander asked.

Linc shook his head, knowing he couldn't let himself go there. It would only make it harder if he knew she desired him, too. But he had no intention of giving his brother ammunition. He hadn't told Xander he wanted Jordan and he wasn't about to.

For the next hour, Linc drank, Xander watched, and they talked about Xander's next book, in the pre-filming and heavy discussion stages. Xander didn't bring up their half-sister or their father again, and Linc was grateful. He wasn't sure why the news had hit him as hard as it had.

Xander obviously had his head on straight about it, but then again, his brother worked his issues out on the page. Linc brooded.

"What do you say we call it a night?" Without waiting for an answer, Xander stood and grabbed the liquor bottle from the desk before Linc could pour more. Which was just as well. He was feeling the effects of how much he'd already had to drink.

Linc picked up his phone to text Max, his driver. "You want a ride back to your place?" he asked his brother.

Xander had a house on Long Island where he retreated when he was deep in work. And for when he came into the city, he had an apartment on the Upper East Side in the same building Linc lived in.

His brother shook his head. "I drove in and I'm going to head back to my house tonight. I want to get to work first thing in the morning. Want me to drop *you* off?"

"It's out of your way and my driver's waiting. I'll talk to you soon."

Linc shut the light, they both grabbed their jackets, and they walked out of the office, taking the elevator downstairs and heading to the city street, where they parted ways. As usual, Manhattan was busy at eight p.m., cars, taxis, and buses clogging the street and honking when another vehicle didn't move fast enough.

Linc's driver was coming around the corner. In no time, Linc was sitting in the back of a town car, fiddling with his phone, his mind on everything he'd learned today. God, he hated his father. Hated the times he'd hear his mother crying while he was growing up, knowing she'd stayed married to her husband for the sake of her children. Linc grimaced. His parents had taught him it wasn't worth having children. What if a relationship went sour? Would his kids have to hear ugly arguing or deal with the pain of divorce? His stomach churned, and he knew it was the combination of the liquor and the memories assaulting him.

He leaned his head against the back seat and closed his eyes, surprised when his phone rang. Lifting the cell from his lap, he glanced at the screen and groaned. Angelica, his ex-girlfriend and one-time friend with benefits, was calling. Though he rarely saw her anymore, he occasionally ran into her at the country club where both of their families belonged.

"Hello?" he asked, planning to keep the conversation short.

"Linc, honey, it's been so long. How are you?" She purred in an obvious attempt to interest him. It didn't work.

How was he? Drunk, pissed, confused, and the last thing he needed or wanted was a woman whose only goal was to marry into his family. When he was younger, he'd had no problem indulging her because they'd both needed the same thing. To be seen with the right person on their arms. These days he was older, wiser, and more discriminating. And not about pedigree or women who faked everything about themselves.

He wanted someone real. Someone like Jordan. Shit, he was drunk.

"Linc?" Angelica asked, her voice causing his eyes to open wider and forcing him to concentrate.

"I'm here. It's been a long day."

"Oh, poor baby. Why don't you come over and I'll pour us some wine. We can work out your frustrations."

He knew her offer came with strings, something he'd discovered when they'd tried the friends-with-benefits route. She'd always wanted and demanded more than he was willing to give. Financially and emotionally. There was a reason he'd been celibate for the last year. His hand didn't demand anything in return.

"Sorry. I'm home for the night," he said, glancing out the window. The car was nearing Jordan's apartment, which he always passed on his way home.

"I could come to you," Angelica offered, the desperation in her tone obvious.

His entire body tensed at the sound. "Sorry, I'm beat. I need to go. Bye."

He disconnected the call, and before he could

think through what he was doing, he leaned forward in his seat. "Max, I had a change of plans," he said and rattled off Jordan's address.

With his mind spinning as much as his head, there was only one person he wanted to be with tonight. The only one who'd understand his pain.

He leaned against the cushioned backrest and waited for the car to come to a stop in front of Jordan's building.

JORDAN CAME HOME and changed into a pair of gray joggers and a tie-dye swing tank-top, an outfit she'd be comfortable wearing to relax and watch television, and also to sleep in once she removed the bottoms. She released her hair from the low ponytail she'd had it in, the last thing she needed to free herself from the constraints of working for Linc's Fortune 500 privately held company, where appearances were important. She was grateful to him for giving her a job where she earned more than she'd ever dreamed when growing up, and she refused to let him down.

She poured herself a small glass of wine and dug into the sushi she'd picked up, nearly inhaling the food because she was starving. Then she cleaned up and settled onto the couch in her living room, pulling a blanket over her and snuggling in.

Man, she'd had a long day.

Since Kenneth Kingston had passed away unexpectedly a few weeks ago, she and Linc had had their hands full catching up on his father's deals and properties. Although no one in the family liked to talk about it, Kenneth Kingston had been suffering from the early stages of dementia when he died. He'd refused to step down from his position as chairman of the company or become a figurehead in the organization he'd founded. All Linc had been able to do was make sure that Wallace Franklin, their chief financial officer and Kenneth's closest friend, was on top of Kenneth's investments.

Now, while Jordan focused on Linc's listings and outstanding contracts, he handled both the business and his father's estate. When necessary, Jordan coordinating with the elder Mr. Kingston's secretary, Suzanne, who Linc had decided to keep on in a different position. He hadn't wanted to fire the woman who'd been with the company for years. Linc thought he was a hard-ass, and they all liked to tease him about his demands, but deep down he had a good heart.

And right now he was hurting.

With a sigh, Jordan picked up the television remote and was about to turn it on when her cell rang. A glance showed her it was her doorman, and she tapped accept, surprised he'd call so late. "Hi, Jerry."

"Miss Greene, Mr. Kingston is here. Should I send him up?"

"Yes, please," she said, rising from her seat, concerned. She disconnected the call.

Why would Linc be here now? When she'd said good night at the office, he'd been drinking with and talking to Xander, filling him in about the sister they hadn't known about. He'd already told Jordan everything about his discovery, and she understood how upsetting he'd found the news.

To show up here now wasn't in character. He was self-contained and kept his emotions to himself, even when he was upset. But she'd never seen him quite as worked up as he'd been about his new sister, Aurora, and her past, growing up in foster homes while he and his siblings had wealth and comfort.

After folding the blanket she'd pulled over herself, she laid it onto the couch before heading to the door, reaching it just as Linc knocked.

She opened it to find him standing, one arm on the doorframe, a sexy vision with his white dress shirt unbuttoned and tie hanging loose around his neck. His silky black hair was mussed from running his fingers through the strands, and a day's worth of scruff graced his gorgeous face.

But his eyes drew her attention most. Devastation looked back at her from his blue gaze with a darker ring around the outer edges.

"Hey," he said, and she caught the whiff of whiskey on his breath.

"Come on in." She stepped back and he entered, brushing past her and leaving her with a hint of his cologne in his wake.

After closing the door, she followed him into her living room. "I'd offer you a drink, but it smells like you've had enough."

Without replying, he threw his body onto the couch she'd been sitting on, choosing her favorite side and he knew it.

"Talk to me," she said, joining him on the cushion next to his and crossing her legs in front of her.

"I'm pissed at my father." He leaned back and groaned.

"I know." She'd spent enough time in their large house growing up.

Enough to know Kenneth Kingston hadn't been a man to be emulated. A man of power? Yes. A kind, caring parent to the children with his wife? Not so much. But a worse husband and definitely a horrible human to the daughter he'd abandoned. Now Linc was left to pick up the pieces.

"Does your mother know about your half-sister?"

He shook his head. "And who do you think has to tell her?"

Linc was close to his mother, as were all his siblings. Despite how long she'd known Melissa Kingston, who liked to be called Melly, Jordan couldn't read her. She'd seen Melly be stern and she'd seen her kind. She'd never treated Jordan badly and had allowed her to come to the house and do homework while her mom finished her day of work. And unlike Mr. Kingston, she never gave Linc a hard time about their friendship, for which Jordan was grateful. One thing was certain. The woman hadn't deserved for her husband to cheat on her.

"You'll handle it," she said, putting a hand on Linc's shoulder.

He pulled her closer until she leaned against him, her head in the crook of his arm. His body was warm, he smelled good, and she did her best to ignore the tingle of awareness inside her. Linc liked to hang out, to snuggle and watch a movie or just talk. Their friendship consisted of everything she'd want with someone she loved deeply except sex and the intimacy that came with it.

So as she sat with his arm around her, comforting him in silence, she ignored the scent of his cologne, masculine and sexy. She tried not to focus on the hard muscled body she leaned against, but it wasn't easy.

She couldn't lie and say she'd never wanted a relationship with Linc, but those days were over. When she was younger, she'd had a crush on him, but her mother had caught on quickly and warned her about their different status in life and how ultimately Jordan didn't fit into his world.

Those words had crushed her young heart, but since her mother cleaned their home, they ultimately made sense, and Jordan had forced herself to focus on being Linc's friend. Eventually, he'd gone to college, the cost fully covered by his family. She had student loans. She'd gotten a job in human resources for a company she'd liked while he'd attended business school.

But maybe she'd read too many romance novels, because her first year out of college, she'd met a hot guy at a bar. Collin had been attentive, taken her number, and called her the next day. They'd begun dating, and she'd quickly learned he'd come from a wealthy family who made their money in hedge funds.

The relationship turned serious fast, but she never met his family, and she'd begun to feel like he was hiding her from his parents. After all, he'd already met hers. And like with Linc, Jordan's mother was wary thanks to Collin's family's wealth, but since she didn't work for them, she hadn't harped on the issue.

Then Jordan had missed her period and a test proved she was pregnant. And Collin Auerbach had panicked and handed her money to get rid of the problem. Much like Linc's father had apparently done to one of his mistresses, as she now knew.

Jordan had thrown him out, ripped up the check, and the man she'd thought she'd marry got engaged to an oil heiress six months later.

As for Jordan, a month into the pregnancy, she'd experienced terrible cramps and heavy bleeding and lost the baby. The pain of remembering always hurt. And who had been there for her? Linc. He'd helped her with her grief and was there as she'd picked up the pieces of her broken heart.

After Linc had graduated business school, he began working at Kingston Enterprises, and he'd all but begged her to become his personal assistant. Something his father hadn't been happy about because she was the help's daughter.

This time she understood she'd never be good enough for anyone with wealth. Fine. She didn't want the upscale, hoity-toity kind of life anyway. She just desired a normal existence with a job she enjoyed, a man she loved, and eventually a family of her own.

She'd taken the job at Kingston Enterprises, refusing to give up a great opportunity because Linc's father was an asshole. Besides, the older man's office had been a long hall away from Linc's. Once she'd been hired, she'd rarely seen him. And she and Linc had fallen into a special work dynamic. She'd be a fool to think about him as anything other than her boss and friend.

A friend she treasured and didn't want to lose by adding sex to their relationship. No more wealthy men for her. Plus she saw the kind of women Linc dated, the type of families they came from, the approval his mother gave those women, all proof her own her mother's words still held true. Jordan wasn't in his league and didn't belong there.

"I need a plan," he said, speaking up out of the blue.

She'd actually thought he'd fallen asleep.

"Do I go meet my sister? Or do I let it go because knowing the truth about her father might be too painful for her?" His words sounded slurred, and he was obviously in no position to talk tonight.

"I think we should discuss this in the morning. You need a clear head to make those kinds of decisions." She pushed herself off him and rose to her feet.

"Stay with me," he said, and when she glanced at him, his lips were set in a little-boy pout.

This was the Linc not many people saw. The vulnerable man beneath the businessman he presented to the world. "You need sleep. Do you have a car waiting?" she asked because he used a driver to get around the city.

"I sent him home." He stretched his feet out on her couch, and she realized he was settling in for the night.

"Kick off your shoes," she said. No way could he sleep on the couch in his work clothes.

He did as she instructed, and his black dress shoes fell to the floor.

"Now take off your tie and shirt so you're comfortable."

"Bossy," he muttered and began to undo the buttons. He worked his way down, revealing his muscled chest and defined abs from time with a professional trainer. He shrugged out of the shirt, struggling with the buttons on the cuffs, but he managed to release them.

Swallowing hard, she took the shirt and tie from him and put them aside, planning to hang them up so they didn't wrinkle even more. He'd need them to wear home in the morning.

Despite herself, she couldn't help but stare at his naked chest. It had been years since they were kids swimming together in his family's pool, and the man in front of her now was a far cry from the boy he'd been.

How could she look at him and not drool? "Do you want to wash up before you settle in for the night?" she asked in a husky voice.

She reached out a hand to help him to his feet, and

without warning, he pulled her forward. She tumbled, twisting herself so she landed on top of his hard body.

"Linc, what are you doing?" She lifted herself up, intending to climb off him when a firm arm around her back locked her in place.

"I need you," he said, his voice full of longing.

His words took her off guard. Heart pounding, she looked up, and his gaze, hazy with alcohol but no less compelling, met hers. Everything inside her twisted with need. Need for this man and everything he was.

"Kiss me, Jordan."

A moan escaped her throat because she wanted desperately to press her lips to his. She stilled, her heart debating with her mind.

Just as she decided to make light of the moment, to treat it as a joke, he cupped the back of her head, and with a little pressure from his hand, her mouth met his. Sparks flew through her body, the warmth and feel of him utter perfection. She sighed, wanting to get closer, and in response, his tongue pushed past her lips and curled around hers.

Unable to stop herself, she slid her hands into his hair and deepened the kiss. His breath tasted malty from alcohol, but nothing mattered except the feel of him devouring her mouth. His other hand slipped beneath the back of her shirt, his large, warm palm covering her skin. Her nipples grew tight, and she rubbed herself against him, enjoying their closeness.

The sound of her phone ringing penetrated her consciousness, popping the desire-filled bubble she'd been in, and brought her out of her fantasy moment. Reality came crashing in, and the reality was, Linc would never cross this line sober. She shouldn't have crossed it at all.

Ignoring the call, she pushed herself up, breaking their connection. With a groan, he met her gaze. "I'm not sorry," he said.

But he would be in the morning. If he even re-membered the kiss. She shook her head, knowing she would never forget.

She stepped to the other end of the sofa, picked up the blanket, and as she draped it over him, a light snore escaped his parted lips.

She gently tucked the knitted covering around him, and because he was sleeping, she leaned down and pressed her lips to his forehead, closing her eyes and savoring his warmth and masculine scent.

Then, with one last glance at the man on her couch, she picked up his clothes and headed to her room alone.

Chapter Two

S UNLIGHT STREAMED THROUGH a window, waking Linc. With a groan, he rolled over and nearly fell off what he quickly realized was a couch. Opening his eyes slowly, he took in his surroundings. Jordan's living room, he thought, and the events of last night came back to him in too vivid detail considering how shitty he felt after overindulging—talking to Xander about their newfound sister, drinking too much, and ending up here.

Not a surprise. Jordan would always take care of him, and she had, as helping him undress and covering him with a blanket so he could sleep had proved.

He was grateful to have her in his life.

Kiss me, Jordan. His words came back to him, floating through his brain. He closed his eyes and recalled gripping the back of her head, pulling her toward him, and kissing her.

He let out a groan. This was why he didn't like to drink. Any loss of control unnerved him, and last night it'd led him to break his most meaningful vow. But the taste of her had been sheer heaven. And despite his drunken state, he remembered how right she'd felt on top of him, her feminine curves pressing into his harder body, and her sensual scent surrounding him.

He lowered his hand and pushed his palm against his aching cock. No way would he embarrass her this morning. Not when he had to apologize for his behavior last night. The last thing he wanted was to lose the woman he leaned on in so many ways.

He pushed himself to his feet and looked around for his shirt. Not finding it, he folded the blanket and set it on the couch before hitting the bathroom. He took care of business, washed up, rummaged through her cabinets, and even found a new toothbrush to use.

From there, he headed to the kitchen and made himself a cup of coffee in her Keurig, and when he heard the sound of her walking to the bathroom, he prepared a mug for her, too. He added some almond milk and sugar the way she liked it and waited.

After a few minutes, she joined him in the kitchen. His gaze fell to her soft cotton sweats and a tank top in a buttery yellow. The material clung to her curves, the outline of her breasts and her perky nipples a sight he forced himself to look away from. For safety's sake, he turned toward the counter to hide the evidence of his thickening arousal.

"How are you feeling this morning?" she asked over a yawn.

"Not too bad. I borrowed a toothbrush." He picked up the coffee he'd made and turned to hand it to her.

"You mean you took a toothbrush. No such thing as borrowing one," she said, her gaze not meeting his.

Shit.

She accepted the mug and breathed in the smell. "Mmm. Thank you."

"It was the least I could do. Want to sit?" He tipped his head toward the small kitchen table nearby.

She nodded and walked ahead of him, giving him a different view, this one of her ass jiggling in the sweats. He tipped his head and prayed for strength, then joined her at the table, pulling out a chair and straddling it so he could face her. Even makeup free, she was beautiful.

"Last night you wanted to discuss what to do with the news about your sister," she said, both hands wrapped around the mug as she took a sip. "I suggested we wait until this morning when you were more coherent. Do you want to talk it through now?"

He knew she was directing the conversation so they didn't have to discuss *them*. He placed his cup on the table and forced himself to look at her. "About last night. I shouldn't have kissed you."

The more he replayed the moment, the more he felt like the man he despised and had promised himself he'd never be like. How many women had his father pushed himself on? Women who worked for him and deserved respect?

She hesitated before answering. "You were drunk and I wasn't. I shouldn't have let things happen between us."

He shook his head, refusing to allow her to shoulder the blame. "I started it and I'm sorry." Sorry he'd put her in an uncomfortable position. But he couldn't regret the kiss, because now he had the memory of it to hold on to.

"Don't give it another thought," she said tightly.

He couldn't read her expression, wondered if he'd somehow hurt her feelings, and searched for something to say to ease things between them.

"Are you hungry?" she asked. "I can make an omelet?"

He shook his head. "Not yet." His stomach wasn't ready for food. "But thanks."

"So ... about your sister," she began.

As subject changes went, it was the right one, and he drew a deep breath. "I want to meet her." He made the sudden decision. "In fact, I want to talk to Xander, Dash, and Chloe, and then I want to give her the inheritance she deserves. And if she agrees, I want to bring her home with me."

Jordan blinked, obviously surprised. "I thought

you were worried that, by meeting you and seeing everything you have, Aurora would discover and resent everything she'd missed out on growing up."

"I was. I am. But I have the power to change the rest of her life for the better, and I intend to."

A slow smile lifted Jordan's lips. "That's the Linc I know. Okay, so what's the plan?" she asked.

"We're going to Florida to meet my sister."

"We?" she asked, her voice rising.

He nodded. "You always have my back and I have yours. And this isn't something I want to face alone."

She cupped her hands around the coffee mug again, lifted it, and took a sip, obviously stalling while she thought about his request. "What about taking Chloe? You know she's upset and would want to come with you."

Considering he had no idea how Aurora would treat them, he didn't want to put his sister in an awkward position until he was sure of their welcome. "I want to protect Chloe. Once we know how Aurora feels about us, I'll let them meet."

Jordan's expression softened but she didn't reply immediately.

"Are you really going to make me beg?" he asked in a teasing voice he knew would get to her. "Because I will. I want you by my side when I meet my new sister."

She rose from her seat. "Are you finished with the coffee?"

He nodded and she scooped up the mug.

"How long are we going for?" she asked, and he released the breath he'd been holding. At least she wasn't going to let his actions last night get between them going forward.

"For as long as it takes to convince Aurora she has family who want her." He paused. "Jordan?"

"Yes?"

"You're really coming?"

Her gaze locked with his. "Have I ever not been there when you need me?"

"No. You're my rock." Though he'd been given a taste of her, he still wasn't about to lose her or screw up their relationship by mixing sex into the equation. No matter how much he wished he could.

★   ★   ★

AFTER LEAVING JORDAN'S, Linc headed home to shower and clean up before going to see his mother. Since there'd been no way to adequately prepare her for the news about his father's bastard daughter, he'd just called and told her he wanted to come for a visit. His mom lived an hour from the city on what his father had liked to call the Kingston Estate, a pompous way of describing the family home in Brookeville, set on four acres of land.

Of course, his dad had kept an apartment in the city he'd used as a place to sleep when he worked late or, as Linc presumed, a way to sleep with his mistresses without his wife finding out. Wanting nothing to do with his father's illicit love nest, Linc had put the apartment on the market within a week of the man's death.

As he neared the exit on the highway, his phone rang, and he took the call on speakerphone. "Hello?"

"Hi," his sister Chloe said.

"Hey. How are you?" Although she worked with him, doing the decorating and staging of the model apartments in the buildings they bought and rented out, he didn't think she was calling to talk about business.

A heavy sigh echoed across the line. "I'm okay, I guess. Still processing," she said.

"Aren't we all?" Memories of how he'd shown up at Jordan's drunk last night came back to him, not that they were ever far from his mind this morning.

The exit came into view and he flipped on the signal.

"Where are you?" Chloe asked.

"Going to break the news to Mom," he said, turning off the exit.

"Why didn't you tell me? I'd have gone with you."

Chloe sounded put out.

He gripped the leather steering wheel of his Range Rover. "Because it's going to be upsetting and I thought I'd spare you."

A frustrated sound came through the speaker. "Linc! You don't need to protect me! I'm a grown woman. I'm getting married soon, remember?"

He winced. He didn't need the reminder of her engagement to the asshole she'd been dating. There was something he disliked about the man. Everything, really. Not to mention, a guy who couldn't give another male a strong handshake was weak, and his sister deserved better.

At thirty-two, Linc was the oldest of the siblings. Then came Xander at twenty-nine, Dash at twenty-seven, and Chloe, the youngest, was twenty-five. Despite his parents' fractured marriage and his father's behavior, clearly they'd had no problem in one area of their lives. Something Linc did not want to think about.

But because of Kenneth's disinterest in the children he'd sired, Linc had always felt like it was his job to look after his siblings.

He shifted his attention back to his sister. "You were upset about the news, and I didn't think you needed to see Mom's reaction. Are we still on for tonight?" he asked, changing the subject.

"Yes. I'll see you at eight," she said.

He'd asked Chloe, Dash, and Xander to meet him at his apartment to discuss Aurora and her place in the family. Dash would go along with whatever they wanted. Their rock star brother was always chill, and Linc didn't sense he'd get an argument from Xander. Chloe definitely wouldn't mind making sure their new sister was provided for.

His phone beeped, indicating another call was on the line. "Gotta take this, Chloe. See you later." He disconnected and switched over, talking to a business associate for the rest of the ride to his mother's.

He had a huge deal pending to buy property on Central Park South and develop an exclusive collection of tower condominium residences he hoped would be one of the most exclusive in the city. The project was Linc's pride and joy, and nothing would stand in the way.

The accountants were going over the properties his father had been involved with, and Linc expected a summary soon. His old man had always been a wild card, doing his own thing and not giving Linc a heads-up on his plans. As a result, the man's death had left Linc with a lot of unknowns and dangling projects he needed to consolidate. His plan was to place Kenneth's deals under Linc's umbrella. Once he had a grasp on everything, then he could assign deals to their managing directors.

He pulled up to the house and stopped the car in front of the gate, punching the code into the keypad. The large metal enclosure opened slowly, an annoyance, as always. But with his mother alone in the house but for the help, Linc appreciated the security the gate provided.

He pulled around the circular drive, parking in front. Then, steeling himself, he climbed out of the SUV and strode to the front door.

To his surprise, his mother answered in person instead of her latest housekeeper. Her dark hair pulled back with a clip on one side, her face made up as always, she looked well. Although she was mourning her husband's death, they hadn't been close nor had they slept in the same bedroom for years. Linc doubted she was truly devastated over his sudden death.

"Linc!" She pulled him into a hug, the scent of her familiar perfume washing over him.

"Hi, Mom." He stepped back and walked inside.

She shut the door behind him and, once in the marble-floored entryway, waited for her to direct him to whichever room she wanted to go.

"Let's sit in the study," she said. "Come." She led him to the room comprised of floor-to-ceiling dark wood bookshelves, a ladder against one wall for show, although he supposed the housekeeper did have to climb it in order to dust the volumes of books.

His mother sat on the delicate sofa with a dark floral pattern, and he settled in beside her.

"So what brings you by? I love to see you, but I could tell from your tone of voice you have something on your mind."

He groaned and ran a hand through his hair. "I do. But before I forget to tell you, I'm going out of town tomorrow. If you need anything, Xander and Chloe are here."

"Oh? Business?" she asked.

"No. It's personal." Dammit, this was hard. Harder than he'd thought it would be. He decided to lay things out the way he'd discovered them.

"I was going through Dad's papers and found checks he'd written monthly for the last nineteen years."

Her gaze flew to his. "Go on."

There was no good way to say it. "Dad had a child with a woman named Tiffany Michaels."

She gasped and raised her hands to cover her open mouth. "She was his secretary," his mother said at last, lowering her hand. "Okay, okay. I can handle this. I shouldn't be surprised, after all. I knew he was having affairs." She pulled in a deep breath and let it out slowly.

"There's more," Linc said. "So I'm just going to

tell you. Dad sent money to Tiffany, but a few years after she had the baby, she gave the child to her mother to raise. Unfortunately, her mother passed away, and the little girl ended up in foster care."

Silence followed his pronouncement, so he continued. "She's in Florida. Miami Beach, to be exact, and I'm going to meet her."

His mother twisted her hands in her lap. "Foster care. Did your father know?"

"According to the private investigator who tracked down her mother, he did." As always, nausea filled him at the thought.

"And they both left her there?" she asked, horrified.

He nodded, glad his mother was upset on Aurora's behalf.

She pressed her hands on her thighs and rose to her feet. "That's awful. Is she okay? The girl?"

"Her name is Aurora," he said. "And I don't know. I instructed the PI not to talk to her directly. I needed to think about how to handle things before doing something rash."

"Like going to meet her?" His mother, who'd been pacing, turned to face him. "You're planning on meeting with a young girl you know nothing about. What if she finds out she's from a wealthy family and decides she wants something from you?"

Linc stood to face his mother. "Well, I already considered the possibility, and I plan to preempt her asking by giving her what she deserves."

She gasped. "You can't! You don't know this girl!"

"I know she's my half-sister. I know because Dad would never have paid monthly to keep her a secret if otherwise. I also know she grew up in a completely tragic way considering her father had enough money to take care of her. And even when he discovered she'd never seen a dime and had been in the system, he didn't give a damn. Someone in this family has to make up for what Dad did, and I intend to be the person who helps her."

His mother folded her arms across her chest and sighed. "You're right. I just…" She shook her head. "I know he was your father, but I hate that bastard."

Stepping close, he wrapped an arm around her and hugged her against him. "I know. And for good reason. But are you going to punish a young girl for his transgressions?"

He knew his mother better than she knew herself. Her initial response had been in frustrated anger at her late husband. Not Aurora.

"So you're okay with all this? Because I'm talking to Xander, Dash, and Chloe tonight and leaving first thing in the morning."

She nodded and stepped away, straightening her

shoulders. "I agree. You're a good man and I'm proud of you, Linc." She touched his cheek with her hand. "Call me and let me know how it goes."

"I will, Mom. Thanks." He let out a relieved breath. He wasn't worried about his siblings, especially since their mother was now on board with him bringing Aurora home and making sure she had the money she needed to start the life she should always have had.

He said goodbye and settled back in his car, pulling out his phone, which had buzzed in his pocket a few times while he was with his mother.

Texts were waiting for him.

Jordan: Private plane booked. Flight plan filed. Takeoff at seven a.m.

Jordan: Sanctuary Suite booked at W Hotel in South Beach. I still think it's unnecessary. Scale down and I'll stay in a regular room.

Jordan: I booked us for a week. Can always extend.

Jordan: Rental car taken care of as well.

He grinned at her professional perfection and typed back.

Linc: Check on the plane. No dice on scaling down. You'll stay in the suite's extra room. My driver will pick you up for the ride to the airport. Don't mention the words Uber or taxi.

Jordan: *Fine.*

Linc: *That's no way to talk to your boss.*

Jordan: *No, but it's how I talk to my best friend. Later. I have work to do.*

With a smile still on his face, he headed back to the office to go over paperwork on the Central Park deal.

★ ★ ★

JORDAN PACKED A bag, not worrying about stuffing everything in a carry-on. If Linc was going to take the corporate jet, she could bring a big bag if she wanted to. Though she'd been with Linc on the plane before when they traveled for business, she'd never gotten used to the luxury.

She zipped her suitcase and set it by the front door, then she grabbed her favorite blazer and slipped it on. Her cell rang, the screen flashing the concierge number downstairs. She picked up and asked the morning person manning the desk to tell Linc's driver she'd be right down.

She locked up her apartment and headed downstairs to find the driver standing by the open car door.

"Hi, Max," she said.

"Good morning, Ms. Greene." He inclined his head, his silvery gray hair slicked back with gel. He'd been working for the Kingston family for as long as she could remember. "Nice day for a flight," he said.

The sun shone above them and clear skies meant no turbulence. "Yes, and I'm grateful."

He took the handle to her luggage and walked around the back of the town car to put the suitcase in the trunk as she climbed into the back seat, where Linc waited. In no time, Max had settled in the front, and they were off to the airport.

"Good morning, sunshine." Linc faced her, eyes covered in aviators that only added to his sex appeal.

Since their kiss, she couldn't deny her attraction to him was stronger than ever. "Good morning."

She took in his white dress shirt, standard wear for him, but today his sleeves were rolled up, revealing his muscular forearms. Thanks to a dedicated workout schedule, he was well-built and solid.

And the scent of his woodsy cologne? Oh, she liked how good he smelled. In fact, she wanted to bury her face in his neck and savor him up close and personal. Again.

She swallowed hard and ignored her body's reaction, happy her light blazer covered her now perky nipples.

"I'm dying for a cup of coffee," she said, smiling as if everything were normal. Before she'd kissed him, she'd put these thoughts so far into the back of her mind they hadn't impacted her daily.

Now though, every time she saw Linc, something about him turned her on.

"We can get some coffee on the plane."

Coffee. Right. She forced her mind back to the mundane and nodded. "I would have had a cup this morning, but I was running late."

"That's not like you," he said, looking at her with concern in his eyes.

She shrugged. "I didn't know what to pack."

Because she was staying in the suite with Linc. First she went back and forth over what nightclothes to put in the suitcase, and then she couldn't decide if she needed a nice dress. Were they going anywhere, or did he plan to hang out with his sister? In the end, Jordan had packed everything she could think of.

He chuckled. "Now you sound like Chloe."

"Are you saying indecision is a female thing?" she challenged him, because she was hungry, uncaffeinated, and irritated with herself for the sudden attraction she felt for her best friend.

He held up his hands. "Whoa. I'm kidding."

"Sorry. I think I just need a nap on the plane." She was about to lean back and close her eyes when her cell rang. A glance at the screen showed *Mom*, and she let out a groan.

"Something wrong?" Linc glanced over as she sent the call to voicemail.

"No, it's my mother and I don't want to take the call." She stuffed her phone back into her purse.

He raised an eyebrow and then it obviously dawned on him. "She's not happy we're going out of town together," he guessed.

Jordan sighed. "That would be an understatement." Although she and her mom had a great relationship, the one thing they disagreed about was her relationship with Linc.

"And she hates our close friendship."

"Also an understatement," she muttered.

"And your father? How does he feel about our friendship?" Linc asked.

She sighed. "At least he doesn't concern himself with things that aren't his business. To him, I have a great job and a good life, and those things make him happy."

Her dad, Patrick, was an electrician who'd worked for the same company for years until he opened his own business. He had job security and he was happy. He let his wife ramble about her feelings, but he didn't take sides.

"As for my mother, don't get me wrong, she thinks you're a great guy. She also thinks about things like station in life." With a shrug, she said, "Me working for you makes sense to her. Our friendship? Not so much."

He winced. "God, she reminds me of my father. At least in how she thinks money defines people. But it only matters what we think. And I know you're good for me."

Reaching out, he grasped her hand and held it tight, something he often did. Touching her hand, her back. All things she'd never allowed herself to notice before.

She smiled at him. "You're good for me, too. Now let's not discuss our parents' old-fashioned views." Even if they made some sense to her, too. "Let's talk about your plans for once we arrive in Florida."

He began tapping his foot against the floor of the car. "I want to go to the offices of Dare Nation." Before she could ask about the office or why he'd want to go there, he explained.

"When I first found out about the paychecks, I hired a PI. He found Tiffany Michaels, the woman my father had been paying. She told him her daughter had gone to foster care after her mother died. Tiffany didn't know anything more," he said, his disgust obvious in his tone. "And after Aurora aged out of the system, any record of her disappeared. Then suddenly, out of nowhere, they got a hit on her name, a paycheck she cashed working for a place called Dare Nation."

While he'd been talking, Jordan Googled Dare Nation on her phone. "A sports agency?"

Linc nodded. "Owned and run by Austin Prescott. He used to be a pro football player. I had the PI do some digging, and it turns out Aurora has been staying with a woman who is close to another Prescott brother and the rest of the family. So if I want to find out about my sister, I need to start with Austin Prescott, Aurora's boss."

Jordan nodded in understanding.

"I made an appointment to see him. I don't want to spring myself on Aurora, so I'll start with Prescott and see what he can tell me about my sister."

The car stopped at a gate for Max to talk to a security guard. Linc handed over his ID and Jordan did the same, a necessity at Teterboro, the main private jet airport for New York City. The airport itself was located in New Jersey.

"We've arrived," Max said as the car came to a stop in front of the main building.

"Thanks, Max," Jordan said.

"Thank you." Linc climbed out of the car and helped her out as Max pulled their luggage from the trunk.

They checked in at the desk inside and headed immediately out to the tarmac to board their jet.

Jordan didn't know what awaited Linc when they reached Florida, but she was glad to be by his side when he found out.

Chapter Three

LINC BRACED HIMSELF as he and Jordan pulled into the parking lot of Dare Nation in the Ford Mustang convertible Jordan had rented for them. He appreciated both her practical and fun sides and enjoyed the convertible in the warmth of Miami. It was a nice change from New York, which still had cooler temperatures.

Jordan had enjoyed it as well, her face tipped up to the sun and the wind as they drove. Having her by his side calmed him, but the closer he'd come to their destination, the more rattled his nerves.

He turned off the engine and faced Jordan. "Ready?"

She treated him to a reassuring smile. "Whenever you are."

Drawing a deep breath, he nodded and stepped out of the car, walking around to her door and helping her out.

A few minutes later, they were led to a desk where a beautiful woman with black hair and red lipstick sat.

"Can I help you?" she asked, looking from him to

Jordan.

"We have an appointment with Austin Prescott," Linc said.

"Mr. Kingston?"

He nodded. "And this is Jordan Greene, my personal assistant."

"Hello," Jordan said.

The woman smiled. "I'm Quinn Stone. It's nice to meet you both." She picked up the phone beside her on the desk and tapped one button. "Austin? Mr. Kingston is here to see you along with his assistant, Jordan Greene." She listened and hung up, glancing at them. "You can go right in."

Linc gestured for Jordan to precede him and stepped forward, opening the door to the office behind the desk. They walked inside, and a tall, muscular man who'd obviously once been an NFL player, a wide receiver for the Miami Thunder, greeted them.

"Mr. Kingston, Ms. Greene. Welcome."

"Please, call me Linc." They shook hands and Jordan did the same.

"Have a seat. Can I get either of you a drink?" He indicated the bar in the corner of the room.

Jordan shook her head. "No, thank you."

"I'm good, thanks," Linc said.

"Before you tell me why you're here, I have a question." Austin spoke as he strode around his desk. "I have a cousin in Florida who is married to Grey Kingston. He used to be the lead guitarist for the band Tangled Royal. Now he's more of a songwriter. Any relation?"

Linc shook his head and laughed. "No, but my brother is Dash Kingston, also a musician, so we're asked that a lot. Mere coincidence."

Austin nodded. "Just curious. Now let's take a seat and you can tell me why you're here. He lowered himself into his chair. "I have to admit when I heard you wanted to see me, I was intrigued. I'm aware of you … well, your family company by reputation."

In other words, he'd taken the appointment due to Linc's name. He could live with that.

Once he and Jordan were settled in chairs across from Austin, he replied. "I came to talk to you about someone who works here. Aurora Michaels."

"What about her?" Austin asked. He didn't flinch or otherwise react, which told Linc what a good negotiator the man must be.

Linc hated discussing personal issues with anyone, let alone strangers, and he resented having to lay out his family skeletons to this man. "I'd really rather tell Aurora myself."

"Yet you came to me first, not her. Why?" Austin pinned him with a direct glare.

Linc sat up straighter in his seat. "Because I'd rather not shock her with news until I learn more about her. I already know she has a relationship with your family, which is why I'm here talking to you."

Austin nodded. Picking up a pen, he rolled it between his palms. "My family is very protective of her, so you're going to have to be more specific about what you want."

Linc gripped the arms of his chair. "You do realize I could walk out this door and call out her name to find her?" he asked, annoyed at being stonewalled.

Jordan put a brief calming hand on his arm, and he forced himself to relax and think. He wanted answers and this man had them. If he was to learn about his sister before meeting her, he had no choice but to open up.

"Fine. I recently discovered Aurora is my half-sister courtesy of my father."

This time Austin didn't hide his shock. "She grew up in foster care and you're just here now? Where was your parent all these years?"

"My father was a bastard," Linc said. And he proceeded to fill Austin in on everything from finding the checks, the surprise bank account, to ultimately tracking down Aurora's mother and then Aurora herself. He had no choice.

The whole time he spoke, Austin rolled his pen, and Jordan subtly slipped her hand back onto Linc's arm. Though he could handle Austin, having her here gave him peace and the strength to dig in to his ugly family truths.

"Jesus," Austin said when Linc had finished his story. "A bastard is right. And Aurora's mother? What kind of human being abandons her child?"

Linc swallowed hard. "My thoughts exactly, which is why I want to fix things."

"So you're here to meet your sister?" Austin asked.

Linc nodded. "Is Aurora here now?" Anticipation built inside him at the prospect of seeing her.

Austin met his gaze. "She's out to lunch with my sister, Brianne."

Linc was disappointed. "I see."

"My brother Braden and his friend Willow have basically taken Aurora in. Made her part of the family. She means a lot to us."

"I'm glad she found good people to help her after the way she grew up, and I appreciate everything you've done for her. But I want to do the same thing. Make her a part of our family and bring her home to New York." To make her feel welcome.

"And I want to check out your story before we drop this bomb on her."

Linc ground his teeth in annoyance. "I flew down here to meet her. Now you're asking me to wait? It's not like she's *your* sister. What gives you the right to make decisions for her?" He rose up from his seat, and Jordan stood, grabbing his arm.

"Linc, you know you'd do the same thing if Austin showed up in New York claiming someone you cared about was his long-lost sister."

The soothing sound of her voice along with the sweet aroma of her floral scent acted as a balm, and the tension riding him eased. Her words calmed him and allowed him to think clearly, and dammit, she was right.

"Fine. We're staying at the W Hotel. Your assistant has my number."

"I'll be in touch." Austin stood and walked them to the door.

Linc waited until they were outside in the parking lot before letting his temper go. "Who does he think he is?" He clenched his hands into tight fists at his sides, wishing he'd given in to the impulse to take a swing at Austin Prescott with his arrogant *I know best* attitude.

Jordan smiled and shook her head, and all the anger seeped out of him.

"You're right." He gave in to her knowing grin. "I would do the same thing if the situation were reversed." He pulled the car keys out of his pocket. "I just don't have to like it." He pressed the button on the key fob and opened the passenger door, waiting as she slid in.

Resting a hand on the top of the windshield, he leaned down. "I'm very glad you came with me."

She tipped her face toward his, her pert nose with freckles wrinkling as she looked up at him, the sun on her skin. "You know I always have your back."

Just as he'd always had hers. So if he needed her now, she would be there.

No questions asked.

AFTER LEAVING DARE Nation, Jordan let Linc brood on the way to the hotel. He needed to get his frustration with Austin Prescott out of his system, and she hoped the convertible ride to the hotel cleared his head. They had time to kill while they waited to hear from Austin, and she refused to let Linc spend all his time making business calls and working. Not when the sun shone outside and they were right near the beach.

They checked in and headed up to their suite. As she stepped inside, the nine-foot ceilings and glass balcony with a view of the ocean struck her first, along with the teal and white décor. A large television was mounted on the wall, and she knew there were two bedrooms, one with a king-size bed, the other with a queen.

"This is gorgeous," she said, walking to the windows and looking at the white sand and blue water.

"It is."

A knock sounded on the door, and Linc let the man with the luggage inside. He set their bags in their respective rooms, not without an argument about Linc wanting her to take the king and her insisting she was fine with the smaller bed. Linc tipped the man, and he left them alone.

"Do you want to take a walk?" she asked, hoping to keep Linc distracted.

He nodded. "Sounds great. Let's change and get comfortable."

A little while later, they were strolling on the sidewalk. She took in the shops. High-end clothing boutiques, trinket stores, and food places lined the street. Her sundress and flat sandals were comfortable, and her hair lifted off her back and shoulders from the light breeze.

Linc walked beside her, sexy as always in his sunglasses and a pair of khaki cargo shorts paired with a light blue collared tee shirt.

"I love the seasons in New York, but I can't say this sucks," she said, glancing up at him.

"Far from it." He grinned and she knew he'd finally unwound.

They walked another few blocks in silence and he spoke again. "You know, when I was telling Austin about my father, I had this thought. I didn't always hate the man. When I was younger, I actually looked up to him."

"I think that's normal," she mused. "Most little kids idolize their parents, and then they become human beings, with flaws and imperfections. Just like us. And we decide whether any of those traits are things we can't accept."

"Makes sense. I drew a hard line at cheating. Hurting my mother. I thought those were the worst things Dad could do until he died and I found out he was a man with a secret he never should have kept."

She nodded. "And you'll never be able to ask him why."

"It's more like I can never ask him *how*. How could he abandon his own child?" He let out a disgusted grunt and they kept walking.

A gelato store was on the corner and she stopped. "Want to get ice cream?" At the thought, her stomach growled.

"Love some. Come on." He held open the door and walked to the counter.

After ordering cones, a mint chocolate chip for him and a chocolate cookie dough for her, they headed outside and were lucky enough to score a small table with two chairs.

They settled in, and she licked the cone, closing

her eyes and moaning at the delicious taste. "God, I love ice cream." She darted her tongue out and slid it over her upper lip to capture the remains.

A low rumble sounded in Linc's throat, and their eyes locked in awareness. Those blue eyes darkened, taking her off guard. He'd never looked at her with sensual awareness before. She didn't count his cloudy drunken gaze. His intense stare focused on her lips, and her body responded, her nipples puckering, and arousal trickled through her veins. Considering her tight dress, he couldn't miss her reaction, and she had no way to hide the evidence.

His eyes slid downward, zeroing in on her chest. Mortified, her cheeks burned, and she took a deliberate bite of the cone to distract herself.

An intense, sharp pain shot to her forehead, and she squeezed her eyes shut tight. "Brain freeze!" she cried, her hands pressing hard against her temple, poking herself where the stabbing continued.

He pulled his chair over to hers. "Are you okay?"

She glanced at him through slitted eyes. "It hurts." Since she was a migraine person to begin with, brain freeze was ridiculously painful and sometimes didn't subside as quickly as it did for other people.

He took the cone from her hand and placed it in the extra cup the girl behind the counter had provided, doing the same with his.

Concern on his face, he held out a hand. "Come here." He pulled her against him, and she rested her head against his shoulder, closing her eyes as she waited for the pain to subside. He pressed his fingers gently into her forehead, massaging the aching spot.

She drew a deep breath and inhaled his familiar and arousing woodsy scent, allowing herself to relax into him.

"Better?" His arm tightened around her.

She nodded, forcing herself to sit up and slide her chair away from his. "I am. Thanks." She blew out a long breath, ignoring the residual pain.

"Do you want any more?" he asked.

She looked at the cone melting into the cup and shook her head. "No." After the unexpected searing pain, she was wary of eating more. She felt guilty about the wasted dessert but knew she wasn't going to risk a real migraine by putting something cold into her mouth.

He rose to his feet and scooped up the uneaten treats, tossing them in the nearby trash. "Come on. Let's go back to the hotel. I have to make some calls and you can lie down for a little while. This isn't a business trip, and if I need anything, I can always let you know."

She nodded. "Sounds good." She could use the break for her headache. The sharp pain had subsided but left a dull throb in its place. And she also needed a breather and time alone, away from Linc and his heady presence.

LINC HUNG UP from his last call. A glance at his phone told him it was almost six p.m., and it had been a long day starting with their early flight to Florida.

While he worked, he'd been constantly aware of Jordan's presence. She'd disappeared into her room to unpack, then returned to sit outside on the terrace, wearing a bikini bathing suit as she walked past him. The scent of coconut sunscreen wafted behind her, leaving him in a painful state of arousal.

He'd set up his laptop at the table by the sliding glass doors, taking advantage of the ocean view. But instead of watching the waves, he'd been distracted by Jordan's sexy curves.

She'd surprised him by ordering them a late lunch, which he ate while on the phone, and she took hers to her lounge chair. She'd remained outside for an hour, then came back in and said she planned to take a shower and lie down for a nap.

Only then had he been able to concentrate on business.

He shut down his laptop and rose to his feet, stretching with a groan. He'd wanted to crash early, but they needed to eat a decent meal. Mr. Chow was downstairs, and if Jordan was in the mood for Asian cuisine, they could eat in the hotel.

He walked to her room and knocked on the closed door. When she didn't answer, he let himself into the darkened room, the only light coming from the sheer drapes covering the sliding glass door leading to the terrace.

She lay on her side, her body covered by the white fluffy hotel robe, her long legs peeking out from beneath the hem. Her hair was damp and her lips slightly parted. He couldn't deny the emotional tug in his heart as he looked at her or the kick of desire rushing through him. None of which was appropriate for a man who valued their relationship above all else. But he was drawn to her in ways well beyond friendship.

He sat down on the edge of the bed and slid the back of his hand over her cheek. "Hey, sleepyhead. Wake up."

Her eyelashes fluttered and her blue eyes met his. "Hey," she murmured. "What time is it?"

"A little after six."

"I guess I needed that nap." She pushed herself up against the pillows behind her, and the sudden move shifted her robe. The tie had loosened in her sleep and the sides parted, revealing the swells of her breasts, creamy skin and full mounds he was dying to hold in his hands.

He cleared his throat and shifted in his seat to alleviate the pressure of his erection against the stiff material of his shorts. "How's your head?" he asked in a gruff voice.

"Better, thanks." She smiled and it reached her eyes, telling him she was okay.

"Good. Are you hungry? Because I was thinking we could go downstairs for dinner." If he could stand without showing her his hard-on, he thought, swallowing a groan.

"I'm starving," she said.

So was he. Starving for her.

He met her gaze, unable to look away or break their connection. She stared back with what started as curiosity and turned to something more the longer it went on. Desire now pulsed hot and heavy through his veins, and from the flush in her cheeks, she felt the same way.

This time they were both sober. And this time they wouldn't stop at a kiss.

"We really shouldn't," she said into the heavy silence surrounding them. Her tongue darted out, sliding over her bottom lip, and he groaned.

"Probably not." Still, he leaned closer. The scent of the hotel shower gel, a different floral aroma than her usual fragrance, reached him and caused his dick to stiffen further.

Her eyes darkened, and she lifted a hand, placing it on his chest but not pushing him away. "But I want to anyway," she whispered.

He swallowed hard. "So do I." Regrets, recriminations, and putting things back together could come after.

Never breaking eye contact, her hands went to her robe and she released the tie, letting the top gape open and giving him a full view of those breasts and peach-colored nipples he was dying to pull into his mouth.

"Take off the robe," he said in a gruff voice he barely recognized.

"I guess that answers one question," she said in a teasing voice. "You're bossy in bed, too." But she didn't hesitate to separate the robe and reveal the rest of her completely naked body.

He sucked in a shallow breath at the sight of her well-groomed pussy.

Then, she sat up and shrugged off the robe, pulling it out from beneath her and tossing it onto the floor. She lay back on the white bedding, her pale skin glowing and her dark hair falling, grazing her shoulders.

"Fuck, Jordan, you're gorgeous."

Her eyes glittered with appreciation. "Thank you.

Now how long do I have to wait to see you?"

"Not long." He undressed, aware of her watching him, her gaze taking in his body and zeroing in on his erect cock. Grasping himself, he pumped his hand up and down his shaft, doing his best to get hold of his desire.

"Linc," she whispered, reaching out and swiping her fingers over the pre-come on the tip.

He jerked at her touch and dove onto the bed, pinning her onto the mattress with his body, his dick pressing against her belly. He consumed her mouth with his, sucking on her tongue and sweeping around inside. Her nails scored down his back, and his hips jerked at the good kind of pain.

He continued to kiss her, pausing to taste her. He trailed his lips over her cheek, nibbled along her jaw, and licked behind her ear until she was writhing and moaning beneath him, but he wasn't finished. Not yet.

Moving downward, he pulled one tight nipple into his mouth and teased her mercilessly, tugging on the tip and grazing it with his teeth. She gripped his head in her hands and yanked on the strands, so he soothed her with gentle laps of his tongue before turning his attention to the neglected breast and giving it the same treatment. Tasting her was the answer to many of his dreams, and he still had more of her to indulge in.

Without giving her warning, he rolled off her and

rose to his feet.

"What are you doing?" She sounded panicked at the thought of him stopping, and he chuckled, grasping her legs and pulling her to the end of the bed.

He lowered himself to his knees. "I'm getting comfortable," he said, and spread her legs wide before settling himself between them. Then, dipping his head, he slid his tongue along her slit and was rewarded with her prolonged moan.

She tasted delicious, and he continued his assault, licking around her folds and teasing her everywhere but where she needed his touch the most. He held her open and dipped his tongue inside her, keeping her legs wide with his hands. Her soft sighs and moans had him pulsing hard, dying to plunge into her and give them both relief.

But first he intended to make her come.

Switching his focus to her clit, he sucked on the tiny bud, and she began writhing on the bed. Never alleviating the pressure, he slipped one finger inside her and began pumping it in and out, her slick walls coating him in her juices, her warmth clasping around him.

"Oh, God." She arched her back, her hips lifting against his mouth, and he inserted a second finger, thrusting faster, the pads of his fingers finding the sweet spot inside her.

He rubbed there and she detonated, coming apart, grinding herself against his face, calling his name.

JORDAN STRUGGLED TO catch her breath as Linc eased up on the bed and helped her slide to the center of the mattress. Tremors still rippled through her, and from the heated look in his eyes, they weren't finished. Which was a good thing, because as hot as her orgasm had been, she still felt empty and needed him inside her.

He lifted himself over her, his erection hot and hard. Enticing. She spread her legs and he nudged against her. She was wet and he'd slide in easily. Except … "Condoms," she said, meeting his gaze.

He stilled. "Shit." He dipped his head and groaned. "I didn't come here expecting to … expecting this."

She swallowed hard. She couldn't believe they'd come this far, and she had a feeling they wouldn't be doing this again. If she let him go now, she'd go home with a whole host of regrets and what-could-have-beens. She'd lose the opportunity to experience one time with Linc.

"I'm not on birth control," she said. "It wasn't good with my migraines."

"It wouldn't matter because I won't skip condoms. Not after what my father did."

Getting his secretary pregnant. She got it. When she'd become pregnant, she'd been careless. She'd been trying the pill, but she'd had a migraine and skipped a day.

"Let me check my Dopp kit." He climbed off the bed, and she watched him go, his firm ass a sight to behold.

When he returned, triumph lit his expression, and he held a foil packet between his fingers. "Success!"

She blew out a relieved breath.

He ripped open the older-looking wrapper, pulled out the condom, and rolled it over his still-solid erection.

Finally he came back, his cock poised at her entrance, and looking at his handsome face had desire pulsing through her again.

"Ready?" he asked, a sexy grin on his face.

"God, yes." She drew up her legs at the same time he thrust hard and deep, filling her completely.

She groaned at the invasion, stars flashing behind her eyelids as she took all of him and adjusted to his size. "God, you feel good."

She hadn't realized how much she needed him just like this. Pulsing inside her, and she wanted to remember him after this was over. She needed him to take her hard. To make her his. At least this once.

"Fucking perfection," he said, as he withdrew and

slid back, testing her wetness.

"I'm good," she assured him. "And I won't break."

His eyes glittered with desire, and he treated her to a brief nod, a sensual smile, and then he began to take her in earnest, pounding into her in a way no man had ever done before.

She raised her hips, meeting him thrust for thrust, wrapping her legs around his waist, and letting him take control, something he was exceptionally good at doing. And he was so good at finding the right spot inside her. Nobody had ever made her come this way. It always took work, more than most men were willing to put in.

Not Linc. Somehow he knew her body already. His strong arms held his upper body as his hips did the work, thrusting into her, taking her, consuming her. With every plunge, his pubic bone ground into her clit and brought her higher and closer to completion. She shut her eyes and gave herself up to sensation. The feel of him overpowering her was heady.

She wasn't prepared when he slid his hand between their lower bodies and pressed his finger against her clit. She gasped and cried out, shocking herself with the sound.

"Oh, God, Linc!"

"Yes," he ground out. "Again. I need to hear you say my name when you come." The pad of his finger rubbed against her, and when she couldn't take another second, he thrust back in, hitting her G-spot and sending her soaring.

"Linc!" She shattered into a million pieces, glorious waves of sensation overtaking her, her orgasm going on and on.

Above her, he pounded into her, seeking his own release, and when he came, he took her up and over once more.

Suddenly he stilled, the sound of his low, guttural groan bringing her back to herself as he collapsed on top of her, his breath labored in her ear.

She wasn't sure how long he remained there, his big body covering hers while they each attempted to catch their breath. Finally he rolled off her, and she felt the loss as he pulled out, and suddenly reality came crashing back.

She'd slept with Linc. Her boss. Her best friend. Her everything. She closed her eyes and tried to pull herself together, searching desperately for the best way to handle things between them now.

What could she say? *Thanks for the best sex ever, no other man will ever compete with how you made me feel, but this can never happen again?*

She winced.

The thought of never experiencing such a sense of overwhelming completeness hit her hard, but what choice did she have? Nothing fundamental between them had changed. He was Linc Kingston, real estate mogul and a man of immense wealth and privilege, and she was his assistant.

She was also his best friend and he was hers, and she didn't want to lose their connection. He'd never had a long-term, serious relationship before. Not one he'd mentioned, anyway.

He typically steered clear of entanglements, and if he ever married, Jordan wouldn't be the woman he chose. Her stomach cramped at the thought of their friendship changing because he found someone he loved, and she pushed aside the painful possibility. With all those thoughts circling around and around in her brain, she was making herself dizzy with anxiety.

Beside her, he removed the condom, wrapped it in a tissue he'd grabbed from the side of the bed, and placed it on the nightstand.

Way before she was ready to face him, he met her gaze.

"That was incredible," she blurted out first and wished she could snatch the words back. Talk about awkward.

He reached out and caressed her cheek. "It sure as hell was."

Relief washed over her at his words, and she leaned into the comforting feel of his touch.

"But you know it can't happen again," he said, his voice gruff.

She blinked at the unexpected words, swallowing the lump in her throat. Although she'd had the same sentiment going through her mind a few seconds before, hearing *him* say it crushed her anyway.

She drew in a deep breath and let it out before answering. "Don't worry. I'm not the type to confuse sex with something more."

The bed still smelled of *them*, and she couldn't lie by his side and stare at him any longer. Turning, she slid off the mattress, bending to grab her robe from the floor.

After wrapping the heavy material around herself, she forced herself to look at him. "We're good," she assured him, hoping saying the words out loud would make them true.

"You sure?" he asked, concern in both his voice and his expression.

She nodded. He'd stretched out on the mattress, and his gorgeous face and muscled body had arousal rising once more.

Nope. Not going to happen.

Shower time, she thought, and walked away, closing herself in the bathroom and locking the door behind her.

SON OF A bitch. What had he been thinking? Linc thought in disgust. The answer was clear. He hadn't been. One look at Jordan, her defenses down from sleep, looking so beautiful, the robe gaping and revealing her gorgeous body, and all rational thought fled. Gone was the man who'd been able to keep their relationship strictly in the friend zone. In its place was a heady desire he hadn't been able to fight.

He knew they were in agreement about where things stood. Their professional relationship and friendship were more important than sexual need. But he hadn't anticipated how good she would feel when he entered her. How perfect her body would mold to his, clasping him in tight, wet heat, cushioning his dick like she was made just for him.

Worse, he hadn't counted on the rush of emotion that had filled him, either. He wasn't supposed to have those kinds of feelings for his best friend.

Linc's views on life and love were complicated. They'd started with his parents, who, to hear his mother tell it, had begun their courtship with love before things had gone wrong. Next came an experience in college that had left Linc bitter and feeling used. And now, becoming aware of his father's affairs and discovering a half-sister courtesy of his dad's cheating with his secretary... Linc shook his head. He was wary of it all.

He'd learned not to believe in the word *love*. To keep to himself except for the occasional need for release or a date to a party. And above all, he counted on his friendship with Jordan. He didn't want anything to mess with their relationship, especially sex. No matter how intense the act between them had been. He hoped he hadn't hurt her feelings by saying they couldn't sleep together again.

He'd have a hard enough time living with his pronouncement.

Chapter Four

PRETENDING YESTERDAY HADN'T happened wasn't easy. After Jordan's escape, Linc had disappeared into his room for a shower of his own. They met up in the sitting area, both dressed and ready to go for dinner as he'd mentioned. They went downstairs to Mr. Chow, where they ate their meal in uncomfortable silence. Never before had she experienced awkwardness around Linc, and it hurt.

Before she left her room for dinner, she'd called housekeeping and asked for her sheets and bedding to be changed prior to her return. She had no desire to torture herself with Linc's scent while she tried to sleep. As it was, sleep hadn't come easily, memories of Linc inside her and their time together torturing her over and over.

She didn't know what today had in store, but she dressed for the Florida heat, putting on a sundress and a pair of strappy sandals. Before she headed to face Linc, she glanced out at the beautiful water and took solace in the deep blue crashing waves. She wished she could dive into the water and swim home. At least she wouldn't have to deal with the morning after full of tense energy. But she couldn't. And she wasn't a coward.

Drawing a deep breath, she walked into the other room, determined to start the day off on a positive note. Linc stood facing the ocean, taking in the same view she'd been enjoying. He wore a pair of fitted jeans and a black shirt with white piping on the sleeves.

"Good morning. Please tell me there's coffee here already? I could really use some," she said in a forced happy tone.

He turned to face her and treated her to the same strained smile. "There is, along with yogurt and muffins. Your favorite." He gestured to the food on the table in the corner.

"Perfect." She strode over to the coffeepot and poured herself a cup, adding milk and sugar.

"How did you sleep?" he asked, concern in his voice.

"Like a baby," she lied, taking a sip. "You?"

He shrugged. "Just fine."

She took another drink of her coffee and the tang was delicious. "Mmm." Those first few sips were always satisfying, and she closed her eyes and moaned.

When she opened them again, Linc was staring, his hot gaze one she recognized from yesterday, when he hovered over her naked body, his erection grazing her sex. She swallowed another sigh that would sound much more erotic than the coffee-driven one.

"What are we doing today?" she asked instead, cup in hand.

"I'm hoping to hear from Austin Prescott." He shoved his hands into his front pants pocket. "Maybe he'll be decent and talk to Aurora quickly since I flew down here to meet her."

But Austin didn't call.

Jordan spent the day by the pool, Linc reluctantly joining her. He wasn't the type who liked to remain idle, and he definitely didn't appreciate being forced to wait when he wanted something. And he wanted to see his sister *now*.

They didn't talk much during the day, and Jordan hoped as time passed normalcy would return. Their clothing didn't help, she in a bikini, he in bathing trunks, his bare chest exposed.

His muscular body grew more tanned as the day went on. She couldn't stop staring, nor did she want to. But she had to admit he did a damned good job of keeping his eyes off of her. And she hated it.

By the time the long day ended and they made their way upstairs to the suite, he was grumbling under his breath.

"Stay calm. Austin will call soon. I'm sure he needs

to break the news to Aurora in the right way," she said.

The elevator doors opened and they stepped into the hall. Only two doors were on this penthouse floor, and they approached their suite.

"Yeah, but you'd think the arrogant bastard would know I'm waiting. This isn't some business deal where you play chicken and see who blinks first. This is people's lives." Linc placed the key card in front of the reader and moved it around. When it didn't work, he tried again. "Son of a bitch!" His raised voice echoed in the hall.

She took her key from her pool bag and turned the correct side toward the reader, and it flashed green immediately. Without a word, he pushed the door open and held it to let her inside.

Instead of listening to him complain or watching him brood, Jordan headed straight for her room and took a shower, washing the sunscreen off her body and shampooing her hair. She deliberately let the conditioner sit for a while, taking her time. Finally she stepped out and dried off, rubbing moisturizer over her arms, chest, and legs.

Since she didn't know their plans yet, she pulled her damp hair back with a headband, slipped on a tank dress, and headed to the sitting room to find Linc pacing the floor, already showered.

Hair damp and slicked back from his face, his tanned skin and the light scruff of beard he left made her heart jump. Stupid. He was her boss and her friend. She had to forget last night.

"Hey." She walked over to him.

"Hi." His eyes raked over her briefly before catching himself and focusing on her face.

Ignoring her pounding pulse, she asked, "Are you hungry? We could order up, you know, in case Austin calls."

He nodded. "Good idea."

"Okay, what are you in the mood for?"

Before he could answer, the phone in his pocket rang. He raised an eyebrow and pulled his cell out, glancing at the screen and nodding at her.

He answered the call. "Hello? Austin? Good to finally hear from you."

Jordan shot Linc a pointed look and shook her head, silently telling him to be nice to the man.

He listened and began to pace the floor. "Yes," he said, then more listening. "She's *what*?" He came to a halt mid-stride. "And you didn't think to mention it yesterday?"

Linc ran an agitated hand through his hair while Jordan wondered what had him so upset.

"Okay. Yes. Of course I won't judge her. Jesus. You just took me off guard. I know how to handle myself," he said, getting worked up again because Austin seemed to assume Linc would be a jerk to his new sister.

"And she knows my father … her father passed away?" he asked, then nodded. "Good. When can I see her?" Silence and then, "I'll be there in thirty minutes. Text me the address," he said and paused. "And thank you. I appreciate it." He disconnected the call and let out a low groan.

Unable to ignore his distress, she walked over and put a hand on his shoulder. "What is it? What's wrong?"

He turned to face her. "Aurora is pregnant."

Jordan blinked, surprise filling her. "Isn't she only nineteen?" She felt for the young girl, knowing what being pregnant and alone felt like. But she'd had Linc … and now so would Aurora.

"Yes. Austin wanted to prepare me before I saw her. Apparently he worried I'd say something to upset or hurt her. Like I'm an asshole," Linc muttered.

"He's looking out for her. Isn't it good that Austin has her best interest at heart?"

He nodded. "It's just hard to deal with the guy. He's got an attitude."

She couldn't control the smirk lifting her lips. "And you don't?"

He let out a laugh, his first since sometime yesterday, breaking the lingering tension. "You're right. I should be grateful to the man and his family."

"What did he say about thirty minutes? Will she see you now?" she asked.

"Yes, and we have to get ready. It's a twenty-minute car ride from here."

He sounded excited and she was happy for him, but she was about to deflate his high. "Linc, this is a big deal. I think you need to see Aurora alone and not overwhelm her with people. I can meet her the next time you get together."

He stilled, his surprise obvious. "What? Why? Aren't you here to be my backup? Or is this because of last night? I thought we were fine. I want you to come with me."

Of course it was about last night. She'd spent the day reminding herself of the reasons they needed to go back to the way things had been between them before sex. And going with him now, making herself seem like she was a part of his family when she met his sister wasn't a good idea. But Jordan had also meant what she said about not overwhelming the young woman.

Jordan forced a smile. "It's about you and Aurora. You two need to meet and bond. No outside influences. I'll be here when you get home and we can talk all about it." She glanced at him and knew he understood.

"Okay. You've got a point," he reluctantly admitted. "I'm going to go get changed."

And she was going to order up dinner and wait for him to return so he could fill her in. Because that's what best friends did.

LINC FOUND HIMSELF in the parking lot of a garden apartment with catwalks overlooking parked cars. According to Austin, Aurora was staying with Willow James, his brother Braden's girlfriend ... sort of. Linc hadn't asked for an explanation.

He shut the engine, drew a deep breath, and headed into the building, took the elevator upstairs, and walked to the apartment number.

Holding his breath, he rang the doorbell. Seconds later, a man whose resemblance to Austin couldn't be mistaken opened the door. With his dark hair and indigo-blue eyes, he was definitely a Prescott.

"Lincoln Kingston?" Braden asked.

Linc inclined his head. "Braden Prescott?"

Braden nodded, extended his hand, and they shook, each with a strong grip.

"Call me Linc," he said.

"Come on in, Linc," Braden said, stepping aside.

Linc entered, his gaze immediately finding his sister and not because her pregnant belly stood out, though it did. Her hair fell over her shoulders, blonde hair similar to Chloe's, long and draping down her back. She wore a light blue maternity top and stared at him in awe.

Braden spoke, breaking their intense study of each other. "This is Willow James, my ... the woman Aurora's been living with recently." Braden extended a hand toward Willow, and she gave Linc a smile and a wave.

He nodded, grateful to her for taking Aurora in. "A pleasure to meet you," Linc said.

"And this is your sister, Aurora Michaels."

Aurora still stared at Linc wide-eyed. No way he could miss the mix of wonder and fear in her eyes and expression.

As if drawn to her and the family resemblance, he walked over and placed his hand beneath her chin. "You have our eyes," he said and pulled her into his arms for a brotherly hug.

As Linc stepped back, he noticed Braden had joined Willow and wound his arm around her waist. Whatever was going on between the two, it was obvious they had a connection, which reminded Linc of Jordan, and he wished she could share this moment with him.

He understood why she wouldn't want to over-whelm his sister, but he sensed there'd been more to her choice not to come. She was pulling away.

"Let's go sit," Willow said and led them to her small living room.

Linc didn't know how she and Aurora shared the space. It had to be cramped, and he couldn't see a pregnant woman sleeping on what he assumed was a pullout sofa. Which meant Willow took the couch and had given Aurora her bedroom. He'd noticed one closed door and the bathroom beside it.

They all looked at each other, and Linc knew he needed to break the awkward silence, but before he could speak, Aurora began peppering him with questions.

"How many brothers and sisters do you have?" she asked. "I mean, do I have? Are they all in New York? What does everyone do?" Unable to lean forward with her large belly, she smiled and sat back in the club chair she'd chosen.

Grateful for her enthusiasm and curiosity, he replied. "I'm the oldest and I run the family company. I'm sure you'll learn a lot more if you decide to come work with me."

"Me?" she said on a squeak. "But I don't have a college degree! I barely graduated high school. And I just started learning office work at Dare Nation. Plus I live in Florida." Panic seemed to raise her voice, but Linc wanted her to know she was welcome at home.

In fact, he wanted her there.

"Why don't you let me tell you some more about the family since I have the distinct feeling you're missing key information?" Realizing she had no idea who Linc's siblings were, he threw a curious glance Willow and Braden's way.

Braden shrugged. "I didn't want to freak her out all at once."

"What's going on?" Aurora asked.

Linc's low chuckle had her opening her eyes wide. "Our brother Xander is an–"

"Xander Kingston. The suspense writer! And he makes movies!" Aurora nearly yelled. "No way!"

"Yes way." Linc grinned. "And Dash is a rock star."

Aurora's eyes were so wide he couldn't help but laugh.

"And Chloe is our sister."

Aurora blinked, tears in her eyes. "I have a sister," she whispered, and Linc's heart swelled because Aurora's having a sister was more important to her than her new brothers' fame.

"How is this my life?" she asked in obvious awe.

Anger at his father rose inside him once more. "It should have been your life sooner. I'm sorry for what my father did, but the minute I found out about you, I began looking. I just couldn't find you until you took a legitimate job that gave me a lead," he said, wanting her to know he hadn't abandoned her the way Kenneth Kingston had.

She shook her head. "I don't understand why you care? I'm an illegitimate child of a man who didn't want me. Aren't you embarrassed by my existence?" she asked softly, her pale skin flushing with her words.

He wanted nothing more than to spare her pain. "I think you'll find we Kingston kids are resilient, and we protect our own. I'm glad you've had support lately," he said, glancing at Willow and Braden. "But do you have plans for once the baby is born?"

"No," she whispered. "I don't have health insurance yet, although Bri said she's submitted the papers. And I didn't know what I'd do about work and someone to watch the baby. I don't have my own apartment. I'm staying here and Willow's been sleeping on the sofa."

She confirmed his hunch, and he hoped Braden grabbed on to that woman, because she had a big heart and was obviously important to him.

Aurora continued. "I can't bring a baby home with me because it's not fair to her–"

Linc glanced at Willow in surprise. Had she put a limit on her generosity?

But Willow shook her head. "Aurora, you can stay until you figure something out. I told you that."

Aurora's damp gaze met hers. "And I appreciate it but we both know this arrangement can't really work. And I can't afford my own place…"

Linc hated how upset she was getting, but before he could react, Willow jumped up from her seat.

She walked over to Aurora and put a hand on her shoulder. "Shh. Calm down, please. Getting worked up isn't good for you or the baby."

"Can I get a word in?" Linc asked.

All eyes turned his way, and though they might not like what he had to say, he intended to lay it out for them anyway.

"We have a variety of solutions in New York. The family estate where my father used to live still has loyal staff who were always good to us growing up." Though he hadn't run the possibility of Aurora moving in there by his mother, he couldn't imagine her turning down someone in need. Especially since she hadn't seemed to blame Aurora for what her husband had done.

"We own apartment buildings around Manhattan," he continued. "Each of us has a trust fund, and I'm working on getting yours set up to atone for how you grew up and everything you've lacked your entire life." He'd already spoken to his siblings about this.

Aurora, to his surprise, started to cry, and he realized he'd overwhelmed her. Something he hadn't planned on doing. He was used to making his plans and, yes, getting his way.

Willow continued to comfort her, and Braden shot him a look mixed with surprise and slight annoyance.

"Can you give her time to process?" he asked. "As much as everything you're offering is the answer to her prayers, she needs to adjust to her new reality."

Linc wanted an answer now, but he understood that wasn't going to happen.

"I realize you want what's best for her, but the few emotional connections she has are here," Braden reminded him.

Linc hesitated, then nodded. Obviously he'd misjudged her attachment to the people here, and though he hated the notion of her remaining in Florida, he had solutions for that possibility, too.

Leaning forward in his seat, he glanced her way. "I could help you find an apartment, a nanny, and get set up here, if that's what you decide. But I also hope you realize your family wants to get to know you. We would like you to be a part of our lives, and I'd rather take you home with me."

Aurora pressed her hand against her forehead. "This is so much so soon. Braden's right. I need to think. And to get to know you more."

He reluctantly accepted that. "How much longer can you fly? In your pregnancy, I mean?"

She lifted her head and shrugged her shoulders. "I never asked. There was no reason to."

"Up to thirty-six weeks," Braden said. "I'm her doctor, though we'd like to find her an obstetrician soon." He met Linc's gaze. "But I'm sure you already ran your own checks on the people in her life and I'm not telling you anything you don't already know."

"Of course I did," Linc muttered.

"She has two weeks before I'd prefer she didn't get on an airplane."

Linc drew a deep breath and nodded. "I'll stay for a week. We'll get to know one another and then you can make a decision. Fair?" he asked.

"Yes. Thank you," Aurora said, obviously relieved. "I'd like that."

"Well, since that's settled, why don't you two make plans for the week, and then I'd say Aurora and the baby need some rest." Braden was obviously as used to making decisions for people he cared about as Linc was.

Braden rose from his seat and looked at Linc. "If you two would like to come to the Thunder football game on Sunday, I can get you box seats," he offered.

Linc had stood as well. "Sounds fun." And an easy way for them to spend time together. "Would you like to go?" he asked Aurora.

She nodded.

"Willow, walk me out? It'll give them time to make plans."

"Thanks," Aurora said to them both.

Braden smiled at her and Willow nodded. "I'll be back in a few minutes," she said.

Linc waited until they were outside before glancing at his sister. Aurora twisted her hands in front of her, clearly nervous.

"So," he said.

She grinned. "So."

"Anything else you want to know? Or to ask me?"

"Trust fund?" She echoed the words back at him. "I grew up with all my things in a garbage bag in case I had to leave one foster home for another. I can't wrap my head around not having to worry about money."

Pain hit Linc in his heart and a lump rose to his throat. Not to mention fury at both of her parents, especially his own father, but he wouldn't make Aurora dwell on what could and should have been.

"Well, you don't have to worry. Not anymore. Which means you can also start to think about your hopes and dreams and what you want to do with your life."

Realizing he was getting ahead of himself, he forced himself to slow down and backpedal. "But for now, let's focus on getting to know each other. What's your favorite food?" he asked, seeking to take the pressure off of her. She looked ready to pass out from shock.

"Pizza. Isn't that everyone's favorite food?" she asked, obviously serious.

He laughed. "Well, it's mine. Pepperoni. How about you?"

"Mushroom and onions. It's been a treat when I had extra money in my pocket." She blushed. "Coffee or tea?" She was getting into the game.

"Coffee. Milk, no sugar. You?"

"Chamomile tea with a drop of milk and sugar. It's been a lifesaver with the heartburn this last trimester."

He remembered when Jordan had been pregnant. Before her miscarriage, she'd begun craving ice cream. She'd practically lived on pints of it until … she'd lost the baby. He shook his head, shocked those memories had come back to him.

He recalled staying with her overnight, hugging her as she cried, and swearing, given the chance, he'd beat her ex senseless.

But Jordan's past wasn't relevant now. The memories, however, reminded him of how solid and valuable their friendship was. Which meant he'd done the right thing by telling her they couldn't act on their attraction again.

"Linc? I said favorite color. Is something wrong?" Aurora asked.

He shook his head. "Sorry. Blue. Yours?

"Yellow." She laughed as the door opened and Willow stepped back inside.

"Am I interrupting?" she asked, shutting the door.

Linc rose to his feet. "Not at all. We were just getting to know each other. Aurora, would you like to spend the day at the hotel tomorrow? You can meet my assistant and best friend, Jordan. We'll go shopping or hang out, whatever you prefer."

She nodded. "Sounds amazing." She pushed herself up from her seat. "Thank you for looking for me. And not giving up until you found me."

He stepped over and hugged her as best he could around her big belly. "You're family."

He said his goodbyes, they exchanged phone numbers, and he promised to pick her up in the morning. Then he headed back to his hotel, where Jordan would be waiting.

JORDAN HEARD THE lock open and Linc push open the door and walk inside.

"Jordan?" he called out.

"Right here." She'd stretched out in the sitting room on the sofa with an ottoman in front of her. On the television was an old comedy she'd been trying and failing to pay attention to.

Pushing herself to a sitting position, she pulled a blanket over her lap and waited for him to join her. He walked in, looking drained but also happy, and her heart skipped a beat.

"So how did it go?" she asked. She'd been dying to know the whole time he was gone, alternating between kicking herself for staying back at the hotel and telling herself she'd done the right thing.

He settled into a chair near the couch and smiled. "She's a great kid. Definitely overwhelmed, with the pregnancy, her life at the moment, and now a new family to wrap her head around. But she seemed open to spending time with me. In fact, I'm picking her up in the morning and bringing her back here so we can all hang out and get to know one another."

"Oh! That's so amazing. I'm so happy for you!" She leaned forward in her seat. "Do you think she'll come back to New York with you?" Jordan knew how important it was to Linc to have his family together.

He rubbed his hands on the top of his jeans, drawing her attention to his strong thighs. "I think it's possible. If she's comfortable with us and relaxes a lot. I said we'd stay for a week, and she was good with my decision."

A week. In this suite with Linc, tortured by their close proximity and all she couldn't have. Of course, she'd be around him if they were home and in the office, but there was something different about Linc in a suit, hot as he was, and this casually dressed Linc sleeping in the room next to hers. Showering while she imagined him naked, water dripping down his skin. Wearing a bathing suit, his chest bare, muscles flexing as she tried not to shamelessly stare.

"Sounds great!" Her voice came out tight and thready. "I'm looking forward to meeting her." At least that much was true.

She would enjoy getting to know his new sister, and Jordan wondered what kind of changes Aurora would bring to the Kingston family.

LINC LEFT THE next morning to pick up Aurora. Jordan stayed in the room, getting ready for the day. They were each doing their best to find their normal footing with one another after their incredible night together, and it wasn't easy. The current awkwardness had never existed before, and he hoped Aurora's arrival would be the icebreaker he and Jordan needed.

Aurora had been chatty on the ride to the hotel, asking questions about New York, the city, where Linc lived, and whether the rest of the family was as eager to meet her as he'd been. He assured her they were.

Jordan joined them for breakfast at a table in the restaurant located off the main part of the lobby. They approached the table, and Jordan greeted them with a smile. She rose and stepped forward to say hello to Aurora.

As she stood, Linc took in her outfit. A cute ruffled skirt hit above the knee, revealing her long legs, a pop of hot-pink polish looked bold and cute on her toenails, and a white tank top hugged her curves.

He drooled at the sight of her, her hair pulled off her face with a headband, putting his focus on her bright pink lips. He groaned and shook his head, wondering if she was torturing him on purpose or if he was just now noticing every little appealing thing about her.

"Aurora," Linc said, his hand lightly on her back. "This is Jordan Greene, my ... best friend and personal assistant." He nearly stumbled over the description and couldn't figure out why when the lines had always been so clear before.

"Jordan, my sister Aurora."

"I am so happy to meet you," Jordan said, pulling Aurora into an awkward hug due to the size of her belly.

When Aurora pulled back, she had a wide smile on her face, obviously thrilled with the warm welcome. "Same here."

"Let's sit." Jordan gestured to the chairs and they each settled into one. "I thought you'd be more comfortable indoors with air conditioning than outside in the heat."

Aurora nodded. "I hate getting hot and sweaty, especially now. I'm so uncomfortable."

"I can only imagine." Jordan smiled, and only Linc knew Aurora's comment had brought up painful memories.

Jordan really *had* no idea what it was like to carry a baby to term and feel the things his sister now did, and Linc understood Jordan's unexpressed pain.

"So what does everyone want for breakfast?" Linc asked, determined to lighten the subject.

Aurora opened the bound menu and scanned the page, her eyes widening before slamming the book closed.

Linc shot Jordan a concerned glance, and she gave him a slight shrug.

"Aurora? What are you having?" he asked.

She swallowed hard. "Umm, just a glass of orange juice. I'm not really hungry."

"But you told me in the car you were starving."

Jordan cleared her throat. "Well, I *am* hungry and I can't decide what I want. If I order pancakes and scrambled eggs, will you share them with me?" she asked Aurora.

His sister's eyes lit up. "Are you sure?"

"Definitely." Jordan shut the menu. "Linc? What

are you having?"

"A vegetable omelet and bacon," he said, wondering what he'd missed.

"I'll be right back," Aurora said, rising from her seat and heading toward what looked like the restrooms in the back.

Linc glanced at Jordan. "Can you explain?"

She nodded. "The prices on the menu freaked her out, and she didn't want to order anything."

He narrowed his gaze, his stomach churning at the possibility Jordan was right. "How did you know what was wrong?"

A soft smile lifted her lips and she leaned forward. "Because I remember the first time you insisted I come with you for lunch to some fancy place you usually went with your family. I took one look at the menu and said I just wanted French fries."

He stilled, recalling the day clearly. "I believed you," he said, horrified by his privilege and ignorance.

"You had no reason not to."

He shook his head, suddenly understanding so much more about Jordan's take on his life and their different upbringings.

"At least now I have an idea about what to look out for with Aurora. I don't ever want her feeling uncomfortable." As he met her stare, regret filled him. "I never wanted you to feel that way either."

She reached out and curled her fingers around his hand. "You can't control everything, Linc. No matter how much you want to. Or how much money you have. As for Aurora, some things are going to take time."

He let out a frustrated groan, but before he could reply, Aurora returned to the table and they enjoyed their time together. They took a walk down the beach and talked before Linc returned her home.

The rest of the week passed quickly, including the football game. Braden had managed tickets for Linc, Jordan, and Aurora, and they'd all had fun. Eventually Aurora agreed to come to New York with them. She understood how much easier her life would be around family and people determined to help her both emotionally and financially. As much as she loved the Prescotts and Willow, Aurora had a deep-seated need for family.

Another plus, Aurora and Jordan had formed a fast bond, and Linc was glad Aurora would have someone she already knew and liked to rely on once in New York. But what was good for Aurora wasn't helpful to Linc. Having Aurora to focus on meant Jordan was able to avoid dealing with him and their relationship.

And he had no idea what to do about it.

Chapter Five

LINC, JORDAN AND Aurora headed to board the private jet for the trip to New York. Linc had to admit he was ready to go home. He had work to catch up with, the upcoming deal to close, and now his sister to get settled.

"Wow! Look at this!" Aurora followed Jordan and Linc onto the plane, awe filling her expression as she entered. "This is really overwhelming."

Jordan smiled. "You'll get used to it one day. For now, though, let's take a seat."

The women settled in beside each other, talking about everything and nothing, but their chatter told Linc coming down here to find his sister had been the right thing to do.

"Linc? Where am I going to stay?" Aurora asked as he sat in his seat across from them.

"With me at least until we figure out a better, more permanent solution," he said.

He hadn't been able to make plans for her before arriving in Florida since he hadn't known if she'd return with him. He intended to talk to his mother about Aurora moving into the family estate.

"Do you have room?" Aurora asked.

He nodded. "I have two bedrooms and we'll sort things out." Soon, because she was very pregnant, he thought.

The flight attendant came over and checked them all. No one wanted something to drink, so she walked away.

He pulled his laptop from his briefcase. As he opened the top, his cell phone rang. He glanced at the screen and saw his CEO Brian Connelly's name.

"Hello," he said as the flight attendant shut the door to the plane. "Brian?"

"Linc, we have a problem."

His stomach clenched. "What's wrong?"

Jordan stopped talking to Aurora, her gaze swinging to his, concern in her eyes.

"We had a visitor today," Brian said. "A lawyer. Apparently right before your father died, he'd gotten himself involved in a deal to purchase land upstate."

Linc pinched the bridge of his nose, feeling a severe headache coming on. Only close family and top people in the company knew Kenneth had been dealing with early-onset dementia for the last year.

Difficult even before the diagnosis, his father had refused to step down or stop doing business in his own company. The only choice Linc had was to assign him a babysitter he knew nothing about. Wallace Franklin, as Kenneth's best friend and the CFO, had been the best suited for the job. He could keep an eye on both his friend and the company's bottom line.

Yet somehow, something had slipped past him.

"Linc?"

"I'm here," he said.

"I hope you're sitting down for this."

At Brian's words, Linc braced himself.

"Kenneth signed papers with a secondary partner, and he's on the hook for big money." Brian paused and Linc's pulse picked up as the meaning sunk in.

"Meaning the company is on the hook. Son of a bitch!" Linc swore worse under his breath.

Jordan stared at him wide-eyed. Aurora seemed uninterested, busy on her iPhone.

"I had no idea, Linc, I swear." Brian's fear for his own position sounded loud and clear. "But I'm looking into it. The lawyer who came by today said he'd have the papers sent over. He's stalling telling me who he represents, which tells me it's going to be a serious problem."

"So what was the purpose of the attorney's visit? To gloat on his client's behalf?" Linc asked.

"He wanted us to know the money was coming due. Failure to pay would mean his client would gain a stake in Kingston Enterprises."

Linc's blood pressure rose even higher. "My father put up the company as collateral?"

Jordan gasped.

"He implied as much. We'll have the paperwork soon. Kenneth didn't leave anything with our lawyers because he was obviously hiding the deal."

The pilot announced they were about to take off, and Linc muttered a curse. "Talk to Wallace," Linc barked into the phone. "Now I need to hang up. I'll be back in New York in a couple of hours." He disconnected the call and hoped he didn't have a stroke midair.

Jordan leaned forward in her seat as much as her seat belt would allow. "What's wrong?"

Linc raised an eyebrow. "Let's just say if my father weren't already dead, I'd dig him up and kill him myself."

"What?" Aurora let out a squeak and Jordan patted her legs.

"Business problems. Nothing to worry about." She turned her gaze back to Linc. "What did he do?"

Leaning back in his seat, Linc glanced at the ceiling, trying to stay calm. At the same time, he heard the start of the plane's engines. "Dear old Dad might have destroyed the entire company."

Whether or not Kenneth's actions proved to be severe depended on *who* his partner was and how reasonable the man would be when it came to getting out of the situation his father had left them in.

"Linc, stay calm. We'll work things out," Jordan assured him.

And because she seemed collected, he took his cue from her and did his best to stay the same way.

LINC BROUGHT AURORA to his apartment straight from the plane and got her settled in before announcing he needed to go to the office. He hated leaving her on her first day in a new state where she knew no one, and Jordan had offered to stay with her. But Aurora insisted Jordan go with him to deal with his work emergency. Linc agreed but not before calling Chloe to come over and meet her new sister so Aurora wouldn't be left alone.

With Aurora taken care of, they headed to the office. Seated in the back of the car with Max driving since he'd picked them up from the airport, Linc filled Jordan in on what Brian, their CEO, had told him.

"And you have no idea who this man is?" she asked.

He shook his head. "Given my father's deteriorating state, I'm not shocked he would do a deal behind my back. The man was a wild card in his healthy days."

And things had only gotten worse after Linc came

on board and excelled in the business. He had no doubt Kenneth Kingston felt threatened. How far would he have gone to prove himself better than his son?

"But Wallace was supposed to be on top of things," Linc said.

Jordan frowned. "I'm going to talk to your father's secretary. If anyone knows what he was up to, it would be Suzanne, and considering you were kind enough to keep her on and give her job security, maybe she'll open up to me."

He glanced at her and once again was struck by how vital she was to both his business and to him personally. "Thank you," he said in a gruff voice. "Jordan, listen. I know things are awkward after—"

She held up a hand. "Nope. We're back to work and everything is fine."

In other words, let it go. The problem was, the more he thought about their night together, the less he wanted to pretend *they* had never happened.

★ ★ ★

JORDAN WOKE UP early Saturday morning with her weekend fully planned.

Astounding everyone, including Jordan, Linc had asked his mother to let Aurora move into her huge estate. The house had seven bedrooms and plenty of room, not to mention a staff available for every need, but the fact remained, Aurora was Kenneth Kingston's illegitimate child.

Yet Melly had agreed. Apparently she was too kind a person to take her husband's sins out on an innocent woman and her unborn baby.

Nervous, Aurora begged Jordan to come with her. Although Chloe planned to meet them there, Aurora felt more connected to Jordan, no doubt because they shared an understanding about how they viewed the world around them and because they'd spent a lot of time together in Florida. Chloe was still new to her and Linc wasn't female.

Jordan had no problem joining them. When Aurora saw the Kingston Estate, she might very well pass out, and she'd need support.

Aurora was silent on the way to Linc's mother's, her few bags loaded in the trunk of the car with Max driving. Linc was on the phone, his frustration growing because they were no closer to discovering who his father had entered into an agreement with. Wallace was MIA.

Nobody had been able to get in touch with him, and from the way this partner's lawyer had dropped the information without details, obviously the man in question was enjoying his silence. Which left Linc worried about who he was as well as the amount of money on the line.

Max drove down a secluded, tree-lined street, turned left into a hidden driveway, and pulled up to a gate, where he opened the back window and Linc punched in a code.

"Oh, God." Aurora's eyes opened wide. "This isn't a house, it's a *mansion*."

Jordan put her hand over the young woman's knee. "Hey, my mother used to be the main house-keeper here. If I can adjust to it, you can."

Aurora whipped her head around in surprise. "You never told me that!"

"It never came up but I'm not ashamed. It's how Linc and I met." The car started up again, and Max drove forward, parking at the top of the driveway, in front of a four-car garage. "But as overwhelming as everything looks, Linc's mother is a wonderful person. I promise this is all going to work out for you."

"I have to go," Linc said to whoever he was talking to. I'll talk to you again on Monday." He disconnected the call and turned to face them. "We're here."

"Obviously." Jordan smiled at a nervous Aurora. "Okay. Let's get you moved in."

They stepped out of the car just as one of the garage doors opened and Melissa Kingston stepped out, looking as elegant as always, her dark hair reaching her shoulders, subtle but perfect makeup on her face.

"Mom, hi." Linc kissed her cheek.

"Hello, honey." She turned to Jordan. "It's been a while. You're looking well. It's good to see you again."

"You, too," Jordan murmured.

Melly's gaze shifted. "And you must be Aurora. Welcome," she said warmly.

Aurora studied Melly, who was a contradiction. On the outside, she was a wealthy socialite, but on the inside, she obviously had a warm heart. The young girl needed to relax enough to see the hidden parts of Linc's mother.

"Hi," Aurora said. "Thank you for your generosity. I know it can't be easy for you to overlook who I am."

Jordan winced.

"Aurora–" Linc started to speak, but Jordan grabbed his arm, indicating he should let the two women find their footing.

Melly stepped over to Aurora. "To me you're a young woman who got a raw deal that wasn't of your own making. My son likes you and wants you to become part of the family." She took Aurora's hand. "So when I say welcome, I mean it. And I can't wait to have a baby around again. It's not like my sons are rushing to give me grandbabies," she said, shooting Linc a pointed look.

"Well, Chloe's getting married, so you can focus on her, too," Linc said, obviously eager to take the spotlight off of him.

"Speaking of Chloe, she can't make it today, but she promised to call you later," Melly said to Aurora. "Now how about we go inside?"

Max picked up the bags and followed them in through the garage and the lower level, with Aurora gaping at the enormity of the mansion and the décor. Aurora had bought suitcases in Florida so she could pack her things and bring them to New York. Max placed those in the bedroom Melly had chosen for Aurora to stay in. Then he excused himself and said he'd be waiting when Linc was ready to head back to the city.

Linc left the women and excused himself to make some calls. The man was constantly working, Jordan thought.

In the half hour they'd been in Aurora's new bedroom, it became clear Melly intended to treat Aurora like a daughter, and the young girl relaxed, becoming more like her normal, talkative self.

It didn't take long for Melly to realize Aurora was sadly lacking in clothing and to take charge of the situation. She announced they were going shopping.

"Jordan, come with us please?" Aurora asked, obviously overwhelmed.

But Aurora needed to get to know Melly, and Melly hadn't extended the invitation.

"I can't," she told Aurora. "I have laundry and things to catch up on at home. But you have fun! I'll check in later, okay?"

Aurora stepped forward and pulled Jordan into an awkward pregnant hug. "You're the best. You've been so good to me."

"You make it easy."

"I'm going to get my handbag and freshen up. I'll be back in a couple of minutes," Melly said, walking out of the room.

Aurora swept her arms around. "Look at this room! It's meant for royalty!"

Taking in the queen-size bed with a gorgeous floral spread in beautiful colors, draperies on the windows and a large television on the wall, a private bathroom and walk-in closet, Jordan had to agree.

"It's gorgeous. There's space for a crib in here, too. Or you can put the baby in the room next door." Jordan turned toward her. "You're going to have to go shopping for baby supplies. But something tells me Melly is going to want to help," Jordan said with a grin.

Aurora sat down on the plush mattress. "She's really sweet. I think I'll be happy here, at least until I can figure out my life."

With a nod, Jordan joined her. She wasn't going to pressure her now with questions she already knew

Aurora had no answers to. "When Melly gets back, I'm going to go find Linc."

"Speaking of Linc, how long have you two been together?" Aurora asked.

"What?" Jordan whipped her head toward Aurora. "We aren't together. We're just friends and I work for him."

Aurora raised her eyebrows. "R-i-i-ght."

"What? Why wouldn't you believe me?" Jordan asked.

Aurora shrugged. "Because you two are close. I've been with you both for over a week now, and I see how you look at each other. How you read each other's mind. Stuff like that."

Dipping her head, Jordan closed her eyes and shook her head. "We're just friends," she insisted. "Look around you. You're overwhelmed by this kind of wealth and they're your family. I don't belong as anything more than his employee and close friend."

"That sounds stupid." Aurora pushed herself up and stood, bracing a hand on her back, her belly protruding in front of her. "It should be about how you feel, not how much money you have. But I get what you mean. I'm not sure I fit in here, either."

Jordan rose. "You will learn to be comfortable," she assured Aurora. "I promise."

"Are you ready?" Melly returned, lipstick touched

up and a Chanel handbag on her arm.

"I'm ready," Aurora said.

"You two go on. I'm going to check my messages and then go find Linc. Aurora, I'll call you tonight." Jordan smiled and watched them go.

Ignoring what Aurora had said about her assessment of Jordan and Linc's relationship, Jordan pulled out her phone, surprised to see a message from a number she didn't recognize. She hit play and discovered it was Suzanne Ashton, Kenneth Kingston's secretary. She'd given the woman her phone number in case she remembered anything about the deal Jordan and Linc were looking into. From the urgency of the voicemail, the woman clearly wanted to talk.

Tapping on the number, Jordan waited and Suzanne picked up.

"Hello, Jordan?" Suzanne said.

"Yes, hi. Did you remember something?"

Suzanne was silent for a moment, then said, "I never forgot but I couldn't talk in the office. I didn't want anyone overhearing and reporting back."

"To who? What's going on?" Jordan asked, sitting back down on the bed.

"You know Kenneth and Wallace Franklin were close, right?" Suzanne asked of Linc's father and the company CFO.

"Yes."

"Well, Wallace was aware of Kenneth's quieter deals. He helped move money and allowed him to do things Linc didn't know about. And this current contractual situation you were asking about? The man Kenneth went into partnership with was Beckett Daniels," Suzanne said. "I didn't want Wallace to know I was revealing information they expected me to keep secret."

"Thank you, Suzanne. The revelation won't be tracked back to you. I promise. And I'm really grateful you called me."

"Of course! Mr. Kingston, Linc, I mean, was good to me. He kept me on and made sure I didn't lose my job after his father died." Suzanne sniffed. "If you have any other questions, don't hesitate to call after office hours."

"I will. And thank you again." Jordan hung up and glanced at the ceiling, trying to put pieces together.

Beckett Daniels. Beck. She knew the name. He was a definite competitor of Linc's in many real estate deals, and they'd gone to college together and had once been close. She'd assumed they had drifted apart. But that's all she knew.

Grabbing her purse, she headed to find Linc and fill him in on what she'd learned.

LINC SAT IN the study behind the desk in the corner. Since his father had had an office on the other side of the house, his mother used this room as her sanctuary, and for some reason, he'd retreated here now when he needed to think clearly.

He could wrap his head around his father doing sneaky deals behind his back. But even with Kenneth's illness, Linc couldn't comprehend him risking the company, and if he had tried to do such a thing, why would Wallace have let him?

No matter who he asked so far, he'd hit a dead end. No one he'd called knew where Wallace had disappeared to, and clearly the person pulling the strings, Kenneth's so-called partner, was keeping Linc dangling. And he wanted to know why.

A knock sounded on the door and he glanced up. "Come on in!"

Jordan opened the door and stepped inside. She was wearing a pair of black leggings and a white boxy cropped top that revealed a strip of skin above the waistband, and one look made him drool. Black Chucks completed the cute, sleek outfit.

"Am I interrupting anything?" she asked.

He shook his head. "No. Come sit." He rose from behind the desk and walked around to join her, lowering himself on the couch.

Her floral scent surrounded him, and he wanted

her in his lap now, his fingers in her hair, her lips on his. Instead he took a look at her face and knew immediately something was wrong.

"What happened? Is there a problem with my mother and Aurora?" he asked, knowing how panicked Aurora had been about meeting Melly.

Jordan shook her head. "God, no. They're like this." She crossed two of her fingers in the air. "But Suzanne Ashton called me."

He stiffened in surprise. "Now? On your cell over the weekend?"

She nodded. "I know who your father's partner is, and you're right about Wallace helping him hide it. And apparently it's not the only secret deal."

Jaw clenched, Linc nodded, glad to know his instincts were right. "Wallace," he muttered. "Okay, and the partner?"

"Beckett Daniels."

Linc jerked in his seat, shock running through him. "Beck," he said, a roaring sound in his ears, and he forced himself to focus.

Beck. Linc's rival in business, but their past worried him more. Beck was clearly still harboring anger and resentment against him, and the bitch of it was, Linc didn't blame him. But a man with an emotional grudge was an unpinned grenade waiting to explode.

Linc had never told anyone what had happened

between him and Beck. His father hadn't known, which meant to Kenneth, Beck had been a convenient person with whom to do business, but to Beck? His father and his illness had made him easy prey to get to Linc.

Nobody but family and trusted people inside the office knew about Kenneth's dementia. Clearly Linc had made wrong choices there. But with his father's more fragile mental state, it would have been easy for Beck to swoop in. But Wallace was supposed to protect them all. Shit. Linc scrubbed his face with his hand. What had Wallace gotten out of the deal?

Jordan's soft hand rested on his arm. "Linc? What is it?"

He didn't know how to tell her. She was his best friend and the person he trusted most, yet he'd kept this from her. Not even his brothers knew. He blew out a long breath, reminding himself if he could trust anyone, it was Jordan.

He just hoped she looked at him the same way after he told her his deepest secret. "It's about Beck. We have history."

She met his gaze. "I know. You went to college together." Bending one leg, she rested her knee on the sofa, settling in.

He let out a groan and decided to get the truth out there and over with. "Okay, here goes. Beck and I were best friends, and late sophomore year, his room was next door to mine."

She raised her eyebrows. "I didn't know you were once close."

Linc nodded. "He was one of the first guys I met. And when you finally get away from your parents and their rules, you go a little crazy. Drinking, parties. Fun. Anyway, by sophomore year I had a girlfriend."

"Lacey," she said. "I remember."

"And Beck had one, too. Her name was Jenna. The four of us hung out together when we could, but Beck was on scholarship and he had to work. A lot."

"I know what that's like," she murmured.

His gut churned but he continued. "Jenna resented the time Beck spent working, but there wasn't anything he could do."

He hesitated and Jordan gave him an encouraging nod. "Go on."

"One weekend, Lacey went home to see her parents. Beck had to work Saturday night and I went to a frat party. I got drunk. I mean completely shit-faced, typical college, lucky-to-remember-anything wasted. When I made it back to my bed, the room was spinning, and I really thought I was going to hurl."

She let out a light laugh. "I can relate more to Beck's working than your partying, but I saw it all the time around me and I understand. What happened?"

He shrugged. "To this day I'm not one-hundred-percent sure. I remember a woman crawling into my bed, telling me she was back and she'd missed me, and then she kissed me. I swear to God I thought it was Lacey and she was home early, that is, if I was thinking at all. What I didn't know or even sense was Jenna had crawled into my bed."

"Oh, no." A horrified expression crossed Jordan's face, and he wanted to die. "You have to know that, sober, I would never cheat. I grew up with my father fucking around. I wouldn't do it. And I sure as hell wouldn't sleep with my friend's girl. But I was so far gone I was still half drunk the next morning. When Beck walked in and Jenna popped up in bed, crying, telling Beck she was sorry, it just happened, I could barely lift my head."

"But he didn't want to hear it," Jordan guessed.

Linc shook his head. "She wanted his attention, and oh, boy, did she get it. Meanwhile, I got a punch in the jaw and would have had a black eye if one of the other guys didn't come in and pull Beck off me. Then, I finally threw up." Linc drew a deep breath and leaned back against the couch. "Needless to say, I lost my best friend and my girlfriend. Beck ditched both me and Jenna, who tried to play the martyr for him, and when that didn't work, she had the gall to attempt to convince me to go out with her." The woman was a psycho.

"Linc, I'm sorry. Why didn't you ever tell me any of this?" Jordan asked.

"Nobody knows and I mean nobody. Would you admit you screwed over your best friend?" He could barely look at her now.

She sighed. "Let me ask you a question to put this into perspective. If a man climbed into bed with a completely drunk woman, pretended to be someone he wasn't, and slept with her, would there be any actual consent? If someone did that to Chloe, would you blame her for sleeping with someone she thought was her boyfriend?"

He lifted his head. "Hell no."

"Right." She pinned him with a determined stare, the one she used when she wanted him to think the same way she did.

And when he thought about his sister in his position, he could look at things differently. "I would consider it rape and I'd beat the shit out of the guy." His hands were already clenched into fists.

She braced her hands on his shoulders, getting his attention again with her touch. "Linc, Jenna set you up. You didn't want to sleep with her. You didn't *agree* to sleep with her."

He appreciated her not calling it rape. He didn't think that was something he could discuss or consider.

"None of that matters since I did the deed. I slept with Beck's girl, and now he clearly somehow managed to partner with my father, and if I can't come up with the money to cover this down payment, Beck will become my partner in my business."

And the more Linc thought about it, the more pissed off he became.

Jordan squeezed his shoulders before dropping her hands. "Listen. He's been holding a grudge for over a decade. It's time for him to get over it. And if it just so happens it was a good business deal? There's no doubt he saw the upside of sticking it to you."

Linc nodded, relieved and grateful Jordan was looking at this from a rational point of view and not thinking he was the scum of the earth he'd thought himself at the time. And had for years after. He'd kicked himself so often, he forgot to think about how he missed Beck as a friend and regretted that things had gone south between them and he'd lost a man he'd once thought of as a brother.

"Since you know who it is, can you go see him and discuss possibilities to fix this without losing a piece of the company?" Jordan asked.

Linc winced. "I can try. But we've been bidding against each other for years without actually having face-to-face contact. But I plan to see what I can do because Dad owes much more than our liquid assets."

A few quiet seconds passed and Jordan finally spoke. "Are you okay?"

He rolled his stiff shoulders. Now that she knew everything, much of the emotional burden had been lifted. But the future of his company was at stake, and he'd be damned if he'd let an old grudge stand in the way of keeping it in the family.

"Linc?" She ran her tongue over her lips, moistening them. Tempting him.

"Yeah." He glanced at Jordan.

She tipped her head to one side, her ponytail brushing her shoulder. "Maybe you can use your father's dementia to declare the contract null and void."

"No." He shook his head. "We agreed to keep the news to the family. If it gets out, any deals he did in the last year, even legitimate ones I knew about, could be undone by someone with regrets taking us to court."

She visibly cringed. "Okay, I understand. So what do you suggest?"

"Either I get Beck to be reasonable ... or I find a way to pay."

Jordan nodded. "So you have a plan."

He shot her a grateful look, once again struck by how vital she was to him. How understanding even when he didn't expect it or think he deserved it. How he couldn't live without her in his life. "Jordan?"

She looked at him, concern in her gaze. "What is it?"

He drew a deep breath. "Thanks for not judging me."

She rolled her eyes. "Don't thank me. I *know* you, Linc. And there is no way you'd deliberately hurt a friend. Or cheat. Discussion closed, okay?"

He was dying to pull her into him and kiss those soft lips, in much more than gratitude. He leaned forward, unsure what he planned, and Jordan jumped up from her seat.

"I vote we go back to the city. I have a ton of laundry and cleaning to do." Cheeks burning, she turned away.

God dammit. What did he need to do to ease her into being comfortable with testing the waters of a relationship? He couldn't stop thinking about their night, their compatibility in all ways, and he wanted to see if they could make a go of things.

Had he done a one-eighty? Yes. But he couldn't imagine another woman who understood him as well or who he desired more.

Chapter Six

J ORDAN ARRIVED AT work early on Monday with a Starbucks grande chai tea latte for herself and a tall dark roast with milk for Linc. She wasn't surprised when he strode in a few minutes after her. He, too, always showed up before nine.

"Good morning," he said, pausing by her desk outside his office.

She smiled. "Good morning to you. Coffee's on your desk."

"Thanks. How was the rest of your weekend?"

She shrugged. "Fine. Busy with the usual. Errands, straightening up, laundry. Claire came over Saturday night," she said of her sister. "We ordered pizza and watched a movie."

"How is your sister?"

Claire hadn't spent as much time at Linc's house when their mom was working. Being older, she'd had a job after school.

"She's good." She looked back at her computer screen.

"So I take it you were too busy to return my calls

or texts?" He propped a hip on the corner of her desk.

His arousing masculine scent, woodsy cologne mixed with a hint of spice, reminded her of why she'd avoided him all weekend. "I answered you. I asked if you needed to talk about work and you said no." So she'd dodged getting back in touch.

He braced a hand on the papers strewn across her desk and leaned close. "What's going on, Jordan?"

She pulled her bottom lip between her teeth and released it. Big mistake. His gaze tracked the movement, his eyes darkening.

"I'm just making sure we have our boundaries set," she said.

He raised an eyebrow. "You're my best friend. My person. We have no boundaries."

Before she could answer, he rose and adjusted his suit jacket. "Any messages?" he asked, back in boss mode after shaking her to her core.

"Not yet but it's early."

He nodded. "Well, you know where to find me." He started for his office and turned back around. "Want to get lunch?"

"I'm going to ask Suzanne to go out to eat. See what else she could tell me." Jordan pointedly didn't discuss specifics in the office.

Approval lit his eyes. "Good. And if she isn't free, we're going to Ocean Prime. Make a reservation and use my name. And if not today, make one for tomorrow."

Her eyes opened wide. Ocean Prime was not a typical business-lunch restaurant. It was a make-an-impression one.

At some point in the last couple of days, Linc had changed their MO, and he hadn't filled her in on why. He was attempting to push beyond the friend zone they'd been in for years, *after* he'd said sex between them couldn't happen again.

As much as she wished things were different, nothing had changed, at least in her mind. She still didn't want sex screwing up their relationship ... pun intended. And she definitely knew she didn't belong in his world.

Aurora's reaction to the Kingston Estate solidified Jordan's feelings, because like Linc's new sister, Jordan could relate to not fitting in. Besides, she still carried the pain caused by Collin hiding his relationship with her from his family, his horrified reaction when he'd gotten her pregnant, and the money he'd offered her to take care of the problem.

She covered her stomach with her hand at the memories, certain she was doing the right thing by putting up a wall. She couldn't handle it if she lost Linc. For any reason.

She settled in to work and had no idea how much

time had passed when a familiar voice interrupted her.

"Hi. Got a minute?"

Jordan glanced up at Chloe Kingston and smiled. "For you? Of course." She pushed aside the keyboard on the desk as Chloe settled into a chair across from her.

Blonde hair and pale skin, in stark contrast to Jordan's darker coloring, Chloe was a beautiful woman with features similar to her mother's, and blue eyes with a darker rim, the same color as Linc's.

"I like your dress," Jordan said, admiring the printed dress with a ruffle above the knee.

Chloe smiled. "Thanks!"

"How's the wedding planning going?"

Her eyes lit up. "Good! I've been so busy with everything. Who sits at what table, packing up my apartment because we're moving in together right after the wedding. I sublet my place, so I'll need to be out and put things somewhere before the big day."

"Is Owen excited, too?" Jordan asked of Chloe's fiancé, Owen Pritchard.

Chloe's eyes dimmed a bit. "It's been hard finding time to see each other lately. He's been working late, so going away for the honeymoon won't hurt him."

Jordan knew the man was a tax attorney and her brothers disliked a lot about him, from his bland personality to the lack of interest in things that were important to Chloe. Her comment merely cemented her siblings' feelings, but Jordan remained silent, as it was none of her business.

"I'm sure it'll all settle down once you're married and live together," she said instead.

Chloe nodded. "I know it will. So I actually came to talk to you for a reason. I was thinking of throwing Aurora a baby shower. Do you think she'd like that?"

"I think she'd love it! And anything I can do to help, let me know."

"I will. Let me see if I can book the country club and find a good date that works for everyone," Chloe said, and Jordan did her best not to cringe at the thought of going to their club. Her times there as an adult hadn't been comfortable.

"Okay, well, I'll get back to you." Chloe pushed herself up from her seat.

"Sounds good."

Chloe headed back to her workspace in the office, and Jordan turned back to her computer. A message from Suzanne agreeing to lunch was in her box and she smiled. A reprieve from Linc's sudden intense interest her, a welcome one. Tomorrow she'd have to deal with him taking her to an expensive restaurant for no good reason. But not today.

LINC SPENT THE morning in a meeting with Brian and, through Zoom, their accountants. They'd found discrepancies in the business accounts. And now that Linc knew Wallace had been helping his father funnel money somewhere to fund deals nobody had been aware of, things began to make sense. Which didn't mean they knew where the missing money had gone.

Linc hired forensic accountants to dig deep, and if Wallace didn't show his face soon, Linc would hire a private investigator to find him, as well. His blood pressure must be sky-high because inside he felt ready to explode in anger and frustration. Wallace had obviously taken advantage of his father's condition. To what end, Linc had no idea, but he was sure the man had filled his pockets with company money, probably taking a cut of whatever Kenneth had going on.

Lunchtime arrived, and Jordan ordered Linc food while she went out to pump Suzanne for information. He took note of the relieved expression on her face when she told him they wouldn't be going out for lunch today.

Fine with him. There was always tomorrow.

He intended to use the free time to his advantage. After finishing his sandwich, he rose and slipped his suit jacket on. It was time to confront Beck. It had been a while since they'd had a civil conversation of any kind, and he sure as hell didn't expect one now.

Over the years, they'd run into each other at charity events and industry functions, but Beck would merely glare. As far as Linc was concerned, he'd already done his mea culpa and had punished himself plenty. He might feel bad but he refused to grovel. His actions back then hadn't been intentional.

Linc never believed the fact that he and Beck ended up in the same business and competing against each other for building and land deals had been part of some master plan of revenge. Beck had always wanted to make money and use real estate to accomplish his goal. But whether this particular deal with Linc's father was simply good business or an opportunity to get back at Linc, he didn't know.

He arrived at Beck's office in Lower Manhattan, his mood foul not just from the issue at hand but the ridiculous amount of traffic Max had hit while driving downtown. Linc hadn't called or made an appointment on purpose, not wanting to give his nemesis time to prepare.

Instructing Max to wait, Linc walked into the entrance, impressed despite himself. Beck owned the entire building, which had a 1930s hotel-like feel, with polished concrete floors, black-steel-framed windows, and brushed brass fixtures. It was glamorous and completely unlike the Kingston Enterprises décor. Linc's offices and the rental models Chloe designed were more traditional than this admittedly cooler look. Chloe had often asked Linc to allow her to mix things up, but he preferred to play it safe when it came to most things. Safe sold.

A doorman directed him to the top floor, where Beck Realty's offices were located. The rest of the building, he rented to other businesses.

Stepping off the elevator, he was facing a grand marble desk with a pretty woman sitting behind it.

"Can I help you?" she asked.

"I'm here to see Mr. Daniels."

The woman met his gaze. "Do you have an appointment, Mr.…?"

"Kingston. Linc Kingston, and no, I don't, but he'll see me." Linc was certain.

Apparently the brunette behind the desk didn't agree, her expression skeptical as she picked up the phone and dialed. "A Mr. Linc Kingston is here to see Mr. Daniels," she said, pursing her red lips. She waited, tapping her nails on the desk. "What? He will?" she asked, obviously surprised. "Thank you."

Glancing up, she said, "Mr. Daniels's secretary will be out in a moment to take you to his office." With that pronouncement, she looked Linc over, now interested in who would get past her to see the king without an appointment.

Linc didn't crack a smile back. He wasn't in the

mood.

Delicate footsteps sounded, and he looked up in time to see another young woman, this one with auburn hair, walking down a hall and stopping at the desk. "Mr. Kingston?"

"Yes."

"Right this way, please." She gestured for him to follow her, and he did, winding his way past other offices and windows with a fabulous view of Manhattan before stopping behind a closed door with Beck's name on it.

"You can go in," she said before taking her seat behind her desk.

Linc drew a deep breath and walked in without knocking first and shut the door behind him. He didn't want an audience for this conversation.

Ready for him, Beck stood behind his desk. "Linc." A smug smirk settled on his face, visible despite the heavy scruff of beard.

"Beck."

"I was sorry to hear about your father," Beck said.

Considering the man stood to gain in Kenneth's absence, Linc wasn't so sure, but since he sounded sincere, Linc nodded. "Thank you."

"Since you're here, I assume you know about our deal." Beck gestured for Linc to sit.

He preferred to stand. "If by *our*, you mean you

and my father, yes. I figured it out despite your attempt to string me along, wondering."

Beck didn't deny it.

"What will it take to make this go away?" Linc asked.

Beck, dressed in dark jeans and a burgundy long-sleeve shirt, another stark contrast to Linc, who wore a suit, tipped his head. "I can't. The contract for the property we agreed to buy is signed. We close in one month. I need your father's share of the money to complete the transaction with the seller."

Linc set his jaw. He had no doubt Beck had the money, or a bank or private lender he could turn to. Linc's money, however, was tied up. He didn't have the kind of liquid cash he'd need to fund his upcoming project and cover his father's stake in Beck's deal. The accountants had made it clear his father had been busy, leaving them cash poor, and right now he was stretched thin with his lenders.

His only option would be to sell property to pay Beck back, but there was no way he could close a deal in time to meet the one-month deadline.

Fuck.

But he refused to let Beck see him sweat. If Beck were someone he trusted with the information about his father's condition, he'd tell him, and maybe they could work together to find a solution.

Linc didn't trust Beck. Not with information and not with his company. "I'll have the money for the closing."

He'd find a way to pay. And then he'd get his hands on the contract and hope like hell he could sell his stake in whatever this deal was so he didn't have to work with Beck on anything.

"Tell me something," Linc said.

Beck folded his arms across his chest. "Yes?"

He studied the man who had once been his close friend. "How did you end up doing a deal with my father?"

Beck walked to his chair, sat down, and kicked his feet up on the desk. Linc got the point. He didn't respect him. Fine. He waited for the explanation he wanted. One he could never get from his father.

"Your old man came to me. He'd heard about this property for sale. Said he wanted a partner who'd go in on it with him. I laid out my terms and he agreed."

Linc stiffened but reminded himself Kenneth hadn't known Linc's history with Beck. The man happened to be someone in the business who Linc's father could turn to in a real estate deal.

"Got all the information you need?" Beck glanced at his watch. "I have a meeting to attend."

Holding on to his temper by a thread, Linc turned and walked out. Not slamming the door behind him took all the self-control Linc could muster.

JORDAN RETURNED FROM lunch, full from good food but without any information to help Linc. She knocked on his door to let him know she was back, but he didn't answer.

After getting settled at her desk, she pulled out her cell to check her messages. There was one from Linc telling her he'd gone to see Beck. The notion made her nervous, and she waited for him to come back and fill her in.

But Linc didn't return to the office, and by the end of the day, Jordan was worried. He hadn't returned her calls or texts, which was unlike him. Chloe had left for the day, so she couldn't ask his sister, so Jordan decided she'd stop by his apartment and check on him.

Because she was on his permanent list, his doorman let her up to his floor on the penthouse level and she knocked. When he didn't answer, she waited and knocked again. Thinking she heard something inside, she banged harder. She waited, impatiently tapping her foot until she finally heard the sound of the lock and the door opened.

Linc stood in the doorway, a towel wrapped around his waist, muscled chest bare, and droplets of water clinging to his skin. Her eyes settled on one particular drop, watching its descent down his pec and over his nipple.

A strangled moan caught in her throat.

"Jordan? What are you doing here?" he asked, obviously surprised by her visit.

Dazed by the sight, she raised her gaze only to find a sexy, knowing smirk on his lips. He absolutely knew how he affected her.

Attempting to remain composed, she cleared her throat. "You haven't answered your phone! I was worried after I realized you went to see Beck and then disappeared."

An apologetic expression crossed his face. "I've been at the gym pounding a bag."

Taking out his frustration, which made her assume his meeting hadn't gone well. "I see."

He stepped backward for her to come in.

She walked past him, the woodsy scent of his cologne surrounding her and heightening her awareness of his nearly naked body. Warmth curled in her belly and her nipples tightened. If not for her light jacket, he'd have visual proof.

Not that he needed it. Her gaze fell to his chest again, then lower to the towel secured by a mere tuck of material with a definite bulge.

"Don't you think you should get dressed?" Her strangled tone betrayed her arousal.

She couldn't help it. She couldn't look at a nearly naked Linc without wanting to wrap herself around him and hold on tight.

His stupid smirk returned. "Am I bothering you?" he asked.

"Lincoln Kingston, go get dressed!" Using the full name he hated because his father had given it to him due to its stature, or so Kenneth Kingston claimed, she pointed in the direction of his bedroom.

Laughing, he walked off, leaving her to make her way to the kitchen and get some water. She took long sips to cool herself down, then rinsed, dried, and put away the glass before heading to the living room.

Linc's apartment was basic in its décor, the way he liked it. Chloe, who specialized in interior design, had helped him turn the penthouse into his masculine haven. A sleek black leather sofa with reclining seats on the ends, a glass table with brass frame in front of it, a matching cocktail table, and what Jordan knew to be a painting bought at auction hanging on the wall behind the couch. Every piece in this room cost more than most people could fathom spending on any one item, yet Jordan didn't love it. She'd prefer a softer, warmer feeling to a place she lived.

"Better?" he asked.

She turned at the sound of Linc's voice. He'd gotten dressed, all right, but he'd put on a pair of gray sweats, his bulge still noticeable, and she swallowed hard. A mouthwatering happy trail and the V-line leading to where the pants tied low on his hips taunted her. Made her think about running her tongue over his warm skin.

Damn him. It was, she thought, the equivalent of her slipping into a sexy piece of lingerie and parading in front of him.

A hint of challenge lit his eyes, and she refused to back down.

"Yes, much better," she said through clenched teeth. "What happened with Beck?"

Linc stalked into the kitchen and she followed.

"He was an arrogant, gloating son of a bitch. But he didn't go looking for a deal with my father. Kenneth brought one to him."

Linc paused by the fridge while she stared in shock.

"Why?"

He lifted his broad shoulders. "I have no fucking clue what made him turn against us." He opened the refrigerator and pulled out a can of Diet Coke. "Want one?"

"Sure."

He handed her a can, then popped the top of his own.

"So what next?" she asked.

He took a drink, the long column of his throat moving up and down. Everything he did became sexual and heightened the awareness he inspired.

"I have to come up with Dad's share of the money for closing or Beck can come after a piece of my company." He finished what was left of the can and slammed it on the granite countertop.

Or, she thought, he could try and reason with Beck by revealing his father's diminished capacity and get the man to back down. But she knew better than to suggest it again. He'd vetoed the idea and he had his reasons. He wanted to protect his company and so did she.

"So what can I do to help?" she asked.

"You can do what you always do. Be there for me." His dark gaze met hers and her hands began to shake, and she placed the can next to his.

Good thing, because he stepped closer, backing her against the counter until she was surrounded by him. His physical strength, his heat, and his scent all wreaked havoc with her mind, common sense, and all rational thought.

He dipped his head and his mouth hovered close to hers. Seconds passed in which she had a choice. An angel on one side begged her to back away. The devil on the other urged her to give in and take what he offered. What her body wanted.

Their breaths mingled and she forgot why she was resisting. In that moment, she couldn't bring herself to care, and she kissed him, her lips meeting his. Nothing about their joining was soft. They came together in a clash of mouths, teeth, and tongue, desire rushing through her as she slid her hands over his bare chest, scoring her nails over his skin.

He groaned, and while devouring her with his mouth, he lifted her skirt, finding her tiny scrap of underwear beneath. He slid a hand over her sex, and a shock of awareness rippled through her.

"Fuck, you're wet," he said, breaking the kiss.

She couldn't deny the truth, and when he rubbed a finger over the material, finding her clit and pressing in, she shattered immediately. Picking up rhythm, he rubbed back and forth as she came, guiding her through and prolonging her unexpected climax.

"Holy shit," she muttered, her legs like jelly when the spasms passed. Only then did she realize Linc held her up, hands now braced on her waist.

Before she could think, she slipped her fingers beneath the waistband of his pants, her hand grasping his cock. He wore no underwear, so her palm wrapped around his bare erection, and she closed her eyes, focusing on the steel of him and the contradicting softness of his skin.

A shudder rippled through him, and a low rumble

sounded from his chest. She gripped tighter and pumped her hand up and down, pausing only to swipe her hand over the creamy fluid on the tip.

"Fuck," he said on a low groan, and at the guttural sound, her sex spasmed and she wanted him. Now.

"Tell me you have a condom." She hooked her thumbs into the waist of his pants and attempted to pull them down.

Instead of answering, he clasped her wrist, halting her movement. "No," he said, sounding tortured.

She opened her eyes in surprise.

"What? Why not?" Her head was spinning from her climax, arousal and his sudden change of mind.

He braced her face in his hands. "Because I want all of you. Not just your body and I won't settle for anything less. And you're not there. Yet."

How had he read her so well? And why was she more pissed with his knowledge of her internally than she was with him denying her sex?

"Fine." She wriggled down her skirt, ignoring the dampness between her legs and the throbbing desire that needed to be filled.

"Hey." Reaching out, he tipped her chin up so she had no choice but to look at him. "Can you tell me you'd thought about how you'd feel after we had sex?"

"No," she snapped, sexually frustrated.

He chuckled and she grew more annoyed. More

with herself than with him, but she wouldn't admit it out loud.

Cell phones rang from the other room. Two contrasting sounds, which meant someone was trying to reach them both.

She shot him a concerned glance, and they raced into the living room.

Jordan was still searching her handbag when Linc spoke. "Aurora's in the hospital. She might be in labor."

Panic seized her, stomach twisting. "It's too soon."

He nodded. "I know. The hospital's near my mother's. It's about an hour from here. Are you ready now?"

"Yes." She didn't care that she was wearing her work clothes.

Within seconds, Linc had called Max, who he kept on standby during the week. They spoke and he turned to her. "He'll be downstairs in fifteen minutes."

Excusing herself, she enclosed herself in the bathroom to wash and clean up. Not caring about her makeup, she splashed cold water on her face and patted off the water with a towel she'd taken from the linen closet in the bathroom.

Looking at herself in the mirror, she saw a woman with flushed cheeks from a surprise orgasm and lingering frustration, but she also saw eyes filled with worry for Aurora. Inside, her stomach was churning and not only with concern for Linc's sister.

She was worried about herself. What was she doing with Linc? Why was she suddenly so attracted to him she couldn't bring herself to listen to her mind and instead responded with her body? She refused to think about whether or not her heart had become involved because that would be a disaster.

As for Linc, he had an agenda. He tempted her, teased her, brought her to climax, and then pulled back because he wanted her more invested than was smart. They were both treading on thin ice with these new dynamics in their relationship, and it scared her to death.

And now she had to go to the hospital and pray Aurora had a healthy early baby and be surrounded by memories of losing her own. No matter how early in the pregnancy Jordan's miscarriage had been, the loss was huge and impacted her to this day. She was grateful she'd have Linc by her side.

Chapter Seven

LINC HAD CHANGED into a pair of jeans and a long-sleeve shirt, meeting up with Jordan in the living room. She still was dressed in work clothes, and he had nothing here for her to wear outside of the apartment.

They rushed downstairs and into the car. He pressed Max to hurry, and the driver made it to the hospital in record time without getting stopped for a speeding ticket.

"Thank you, Max. I really appreciate it," Linc said as he helped Jordan out of the car.

"Good luck," Max replied.

They rushed into the hospital and were directed to the maternity ward, where Linc found his mother in the waiting room, pacing the floor. There were no other people present.

"Mom."

She rushed over and wrapped her arms around him, accepting his hug before stepping back. "I don't know what happened. We ate dinner. She said she was exhausted and went up to her room. Then I heard her cry for me. She was doubled over and her water had broken." Glancing at Linc, then Jordan, his mother had tears in her eyes.

"She's thirty-six and a half weeks, right?" Jordan asked.

Linc did the mental math. Braden Prescott had said she had two weeks to travel. They had stayed in Florida with her for a week, and it had been about another week and a half here in New York.

"Yes," his mom said. "And the baby can be born healthy. As long as the lungs are developed and the digestive system is okay, everything will be fine."

Linc blew out a deep breath. "Then we'll believe everything is going to be okay. The power of positive thinking, right?"

Both Jordan and his mother nodded, but Linc knew they were all still shaken.

"Is Aurora alone?" Jordan asked.

"They put her in a wheelchair and took her away." His mom wrung her hands, and Linc glanced at Jordan, giving her a slight nod.

She rushed out of the waiting room, and Linc knew she'd insist on seeing Aurora or at least getting someone to ask Aurora if she wanted Jordan with her during delivery. She shouldn't be alone. No way would she want Linc with her, and his mother didn't seem inclined to want to be part of the birth. That left

Jordan.

"Come on, Mom. Let's sit." Linc led his mother to a chair, and they settled in to wait.

As time passed, he kicked his feet out and glanced at the old, cracked ceiling. His phone buzzed with a text from Jordan, letting him know she was with Aurora and staying. And the baby should be born soon because Aurora was already eight centimeters dilated.

Of course, his thoughts turned to Jordan in the delivery room. His heart hurt for her, knowing the memories and might-have-beens he was certain were going through her mind.

Linc wasn't good at waiting, and he kept glancing at the time on his phone and the clock on the wall. Neither seemed to move. His mother put her head on his shoulder and dozed while he leaned his head back against the wall and shut his eyes.

"Linc!" Jordan's voice woke him. He raised his head and the weight of his mother lifted from his shoulder.

"How is she?" his mom asked.

"Aurora is great." Jordan smiled wide, her cheeks flushed, eyes gleaming. "And she had a healthy baby girl. Six point one pounds and eighteen inches!"

"Oh, that's wonderful!" His mom rose to her feet and Linc followed. "I'm so relieved." She glanced up at him. "Now that we have news, I'm going to the ladies' room. Maybe after, we can see them."

Linc grinned. "Go ahead. I'll wait for you." He paused until his mother had walked out before turning to Jordan and placing his hands on her shoulders. "You okay?"

"It was amazing, Linc. A true miracle. And she's so lucky there were no issues with the early delivery." She smiled wide. "And the baby is precious. You have a niece!"

Relief rushed through him that everyone, including Jordan, it seemed, was fine. "When can we see them?"

"They just want to get her settled in a room."

Something dawned on him and he said, "I'm going to make sure she has a private room."

Jordan shook her head and rolled her eyes. "Of course you are."

He laughed at her reaction. "She's a Kingston, isn't she?"

A little while later, after Linc had paid for a private room for his new sister, they were all there, the baby in Aurora's arms. He had no doubt if he hadn't thrown his weight around with the hospital, not only paying for a private room but making a big donation, they all wouldn't be allowed in. They were given leeway, which was what he'd wanted.

"How are you?" his mom asked her.

"I'm tired and sore." Aurora glanced at Linc and blushed.

Yeah, he didn't want to think about the details either.

"But happy," she continued. "I thought I'd be alone and afraid and have nowhere to go after I had this baby. I didn't know if I'd have to give her up." Her eyes watered and she pulled the infant closer. "But thanks to you all ... I just feel so lucky."

Walking over, his mom brushed a hand over Aurora's hair, much as she'd do if it where Chloe lying in the bed. "You're not alone and you never will be."

God, Linc loved his mother. She took a shitty situation, her husband's mistress's child, and brought her into the family easily. When she looked at Aurora, she only saw a young woman in need. And Linc admired her.

Jordan stood by his side, and not giving a damn who saw, he wrapped an arm around her and pulled her close, wanting to share this moment with her.

"Does anyone want to hold her?" Aurora offered.

"I do but since Jordan was there for the big event, I think she should get the honors," his mom said.

Beside him, Jordan stiffened. "It's okay, Melly. You go ahead."

Linc tugged her into him and she didn't try and pull away.

His mom smiled and was soon sitting with the infant in her arms.

"Have you thought of a name?" Linc asked.

Aurora shook her head. "Not yet. I figured I had more time."

"It will come to you."

Melly cooed at the baby and eventually looked up. "Jordan, come. You should hold her, too."

His mother had no idea about Jordan's past or her miscarriage, had no idea this might be bringing up painful emotions for her.

"Mom—"

"I'd love to," Jordan said, pulling out of his embrace. She took the chair next to his mother, and they carefully transferred the infant.

He watched her every move as she gently held the baby, cradling her in her arms and cushioning her head. With one hand, she moved the pink swaddling away from her cheek and looked at her tiny face.

Tears pooled in Jordan's eyes and only Linc knew why. Only he understood the depths of both her personal pain and her joy for Aurora.

A lump rose to his throat as he studied her, and he made a decision. As soon as Chloe and Xander arrived, he was taking Jordan home. And not back to her apartment as he felt certain she'd insist he do.

She'd been there for his sister and he'd be there for

her now.

BY THE TIME Jordan and Linc were in the car on their way home from the hospital, Jordan was both mentally and physically exhausted. Linc seemed to understand, because he let her sit in silence on the drive and process her feelings.

Holding Aurora's hand during the entire birth had been both exhilarating and draining. The emotional impact of watching something she hadn't gotten to do, and then cradling the baby? At this point she was numb.

She must have fallen asleep, because she woke to the sound of the car slowing, and she sat up, assuming they'd reached her apartment.

"Are we at my place?" she asked.

"Thanks, Max," Linc said, opening the door.

He hadn't answered her question, but she slid out and accepted his hand, letting him pull her out … in front of his building.

"Wait. Why didn't you take me home?" She dug in her heels.

Literally.

She was still wearing pumps after a day at work, and she'd had them on for much of her time at the hospital. To say she was ready to keel over was an understatement.

"Because you had a long day and you shouldn't be alone." Linc placed a hand on her lower back to guide her inside.

She blinked up at him. "Did you think about asking me?"

"Nope. I thought about taking care of you. Let's go." He nudged her forward.

With a groan, she went along to his apartment, at this point not caring where she got off her feet as long as she did just that.

Once he let them inside, she turned. "I'm going to take Aurora's old room."

He raised his gaze. Then without warning, scooped her into his arms and walked toward his bedroom. "I said I wanted to take care of you, so let me."

Too tired to fight, she wrapped an arm around his neck to steady herself and held on until he lowered her onto his bed. She immediately kicked off her heels and groaned in relief.

He strode to his massive walk-in closet, which had drawers as well as hanging room, and returned with a gray tee shirt, and she accepted it gratefully.

"I'll leave a toothbrush and towels in the bathroom. You can do what you need to while I order us something for dinner. Unless you'd rather go to sleep?"

"Pizza," she said at the same time her stomach let out a very unladylike growl. Laughing, she folded her arms over her belly. "A large one please."

He laughed and nodded. "I'll be in the living room."

Grateful for the privacy, she scooted off the bed and headed for the bathroom, where she changed into his shirt, which was huge, hung to her thighs, and smelled like his laundry detergent. Of course, it reminded her of him, and she lifted it to her nose and inhaled deeply. She splashed cold water on her face and washed up as best she could, borrowing his deodorant and brushing her teeth.

She had no idea if he expected her to sleep in his bed, and she was too tired to deal with the question now. In fact, she was too tired to fight it later. All she wanted was a full stomach and a comfortable bed.

The pizza arrived quickly, and she ate it equally fast, not the least bit embarrassed about the three slices she devoured because it was Linc. And he'd never judged her before.

Once they finished, she stretched her hands over her head and yawned. Too late, she realized the action pulled the shirt against her braless breasts.

His gaze zeroed in on where her nipples pushed against the soft material, and his eyes dilated with awareness and need. "Why don't you go lie down?" he asked in a gruff tone. "I'll be there in a little while."

She swallowed back the argument that automatically rose, because if she looked deep, she didn't want to be alone. She wanted to lie down in Linc's big bed and let him comfort her while she fell asleep.

"Okay, thanks. I will." After padding into his room, slowly wilting, she brushed her teeth again because she was getting into bed with Linc, turned down the covers, crawled onto the mattress, and immediately passed out.

SOMETHING WARM AND heavy cushioned Jordan in suffocating heat. She adjusted herself and tried to push off the comforter, but a hard barrier stopped her. She blinked and remembered. She was in Linc's bed, and his arm was wrapped securely around her, holding the covers in place.

She attempted to wriggle free and he clamped his arm tighter.

"Going somewhere?" he asked in a morning-roughened voice.

A sexy gruff voice that had her relaxing back into him. Morning wood stood stiff against her lower back, and she moaned at the feel of his sizeable erection.

She closed her eyes and accepted the inevitable. She couldn't resist him and didn't want to, and knowing she was done fighting, at least for now, she rolled within his embrace and turned to face him.

A light coating of beard covered his face, and she ran her hand over the stubble. "I like the scruffy look," she murmured.

He caught her wrist in his hand. "I like waking up to you in my bed."

She couldn't hold back her smile. "I'm not going to give you a hard time for bringing me here. And I'm not going to fight us. Not right now."

"What changed?" he asked, clearly needing to understand.

She sighed. "I can't deny the attraction between us, and it's taking too much out of me to try." Biting down on her lower lip, she wondered how deep to delve, how much of herself to give.

In the end, she couldn't be anything but honest. "Last night was emotional, and you understood without my having to explain." It had broken down her defenses and put her in a place where she was willing to act on their mutual need.

"Well, I'm glad."

She swallowed hard. She didn't know what the future held, and yes, thinking of things imploding and changing scared her. But she wasn't willing to walk away from him now. "Do you really want to waste time talking?" she asked.

He treated her to his sexiest grin. "Hell no." And then he pounced, his big body coming over hers and capturing her beneath him.

As she wound her arms around his neck, his mouth came down on hers. He kissed her long and hard. He kissed her like his life depended on it. And she returned the sentiment, teasing back with her tongue, nipping with her teeth, dragging her nails down his back as their bodies ground together.

He lifted his head, drew in a harsh breath, and sat up so he could wrangle her tee shirt over her hips, her torso, and as she raised her arms, he was able to complete his mission. He flung the shirt onto the floor, leaving her naked except for her underwear. She wriggled them off, then pushed herself farther up on the bed. Meanwhile, he'd hopped off and stripped off his boxer briefs.

She glanced at his thick cock, hard and ready for her, and a moan left her throat.

Hearing the sound, he grinned before pulling open his nightstand and retrieving a condom, ripping it open, and gliding the covering over his erection.

He returned, climbing onto the bed and brushing a roughened fingertip over her nipple. Her pussy spasmed and her hips arched off the mattress.

"You're gorgeous," he said, desire glittering in his eyes. "And I want you more than I've ever wanted anything in my life."

She opened her eyes wide. Before she could otherwise react, he spoke. "Up and on your knees, baby."

At his domineering tone, her nipples hardened, and she had no problem obeying. If she was going to give up the fight, she would enjoy every last minute.

She turned and settled on all fours, her entire body humming with anticipation even as she wondered why he'd positioned her this way. Maybe he just liked it. Or, knowing Linc, maybe he sensed she didn't want to see him face-to-face and add to the emotional overload she'd experienced. Regardless of why, she'd take it.

He came behind her, the heat of his big body tempting as he wrapped around her. He slid a finger over the bumps in her spine, causing her to tremble and arch beneath his hand as he teased her.

Without warning, he poised his erection at her opening, one hand grasping her hips. "Hold on," he warned, and she held her breath as he thrust deep inside her.

She groaned, filled up, body quivering and, dammit, her emotions engaged. Closing her eyes, she fought past the lump in her throat and focused on the sensations overtaking her every time Linc pulled out and slammed back in. Over and over. And like last time, he knew her body, hitting the right spot.

"Oh, damn, Linc. Harder."

His fingers squeezed her side tighter, and he did as she asked. He took her with a steady rhythm, hammering into her until she forgot where they were, her name, everything but the building euphoria inside her and the knowledge it was Linc causing the feelings.

Slipping his hand farther around her, his fingers found her clit and strummed the tight bud until she exploded, her body stiffening as the waves kept pummeling her. Linc kept up the stroking until she was wrung dry. Then he thrust in and out, hard, fast, until he found his release.

They collapsed together onto the bed, her breathing ragged, his coming in desperate gulps. Finally he rose and disappeared into the bathroom, returning quickly.

He pulled down the covers and helped her climb beneath them. Although she was sticky between her thighs, she didn't care as she snuggled against him. For now, wrapped in his arms, she felt safe. And wanted to hold on to those feelings while she could.

LINC HELD JORDAN in his arms, silence surrounding them. He buried his face in her hair and inhaled her fragrant scent. She'd taken him by surprise and though he'd planned to join her in bed and urge her to talk about her feelings, he hadn't been able to deny her what they both needed. But with their physical desires sated, it was time to deal with her past.

"You okay?" he asked.

"Amazing," she murmured. "Want to do it again?"

He let out a low chuckle. "Later. Right now I want to talk." His cock didn't like that answer, and from the way Jordan stiffened, neither did she. But he wasn't going to let her ignore him.

Rolling her onto her back, he propped an arm up, and lying on his side, he met her gaze. If he had to wait an hour for her to respond, he would.

"About what?" she asked at last.

"How you felt being with Aurora last night. Watching her give birth. Holding the baby. I don't want you to bury it all inside. It's not good for you."

She shifted toward him and her big blue eyes met his. "I was happy for her, of course."

He shook his head. "That's not what I meant and you know it."

Her sigh echoed around the room. "It hurt. Is that what you want to hear?"

"I want to hear the truth." And then he intended to comfort her.

Closing her eyes in resignation, she began to speak. "Back when I found out I was pregnant, I was petrified. I mean, I'd had a plan. Go to college, find a job, and make money supporting myself in the business world. All of a sudden, those plans were in jeopardy. The baby's father, my boyfriend, wanted nothing to do with us. And there might have been a time or two I wished it hadn't happened." A tear leaked out of her eye, and Linc brushed it away with his thumb.

Her eyelashes fluttered and she looked at him. "But I never meant I wanted to lose my baby." Her voice cut off, a choking sound coming from her throat.

"I know that," he rushed to assure her. He'd never once thought she blamed herself for her miscarriage. Needing to touch her, he pulled her back into his arms. "And it wasn't your fault."

"Mentally I know but in my heart I feel guilty."

He stroked her hair as she gathered the courage to continue.

"I was so happy for Aurora," she said into his chest, moisture from her tears coating his skin. "But at the same time, I was faced with what I lost."

He held her as she let out the pain she'd been holding back while being strong for Aurora.

After a while, her trembling subsided and she pulled back. "I'm okay. Thank you." Her cheeks were red, her eyes glassy, but she wasn't an ugly crier. In fact, she was appealing with her heart out there for him to see.

"I hope you feel lighter," he said.

She nodded. "But don't expect me to thank you," she said with a wry twist of her lips.

"Wouldn't dream of it." He let out a low laugh and then decided they'd had all the discussion she needed.

Lying beside him, he breathed in the mixed scent of sex and her floral fragrance and he got hard all over again. She met his gaze, and he saw the second she became aware of his renewed desire. Her cheeks flushed, her eyes dilated, and suddenly they were on the same page.

She pressed his shoulders back and crawled on top of him, sealing her mouth over his. No way would he argue. He grasped the back of her neck, holding her in place as they kissed, her soft, wet pussy sliding over his abdomen.

"Fuck," he muttered, breaking their kiss, his focus on the warm feel. "Grab a condom," he told her. "Top drawer."

She reached over and pulled out protection from the partially open drawer, tearing the packet open, and settled back over his lower body.

Wearing nothing but a sexy smile, she wrapped her slender fingers around his erection and worked the condom over his hard length. She took her time, and he gritted his teeth against the teasing she subjected him to. Then, rising up on her knees, she gripped his cock in her hand and positioned him at her entrance.

"You're torturing me," he said, his jaw clenched tight.

She shook her head, her long dark hair flowing around her shoulders. "I'm enjoying touching you," she said, her grip tightening at the base of his shaft. Slowly, she worked herself over him, her slick body tightening as she took him deeper inside her.

Letting her be in control was killing him. He wanted nothing more than to take over and pump his hips up and down until he exploded, bringing her with him. But she seemed to need this. Seemed to want the power, and after the emotional break she hadn't been able to control earlier, the one he'd pushed her to experience, he needed to give her this now. Even if it killed him to wait.

Finally she let go, her legs collapsing, her sweet pussy engulfing him in heat.

"F-u-u-ck," he said, pulling in a deep breath.

"That's what I'm trying to do." She laughed, squeezing his dick tighter as she did.

And he lost his ability to wait. "Ride me or I'm going to flip you over and fuck you hard." It was a promise, not a threat.

"Do it." Her eyes dilated and her words shocked him, but he didn't doubt her sincerity or the way her body pulsed around him.

Without breaking their physical connection, he managed to switch their positions and take her hard and fast. But hard and fast didn't negate how much he felt, how what they shared was unique and nothing like he'd experienced with any other woman. Because Jordan was special.

And when she wrapped her legs around his waist and gave herself over, his name on her lips, her orgasm triggered his own. He came hard and fast, aware only of the woman beneath him and how perfect she made him feel.

JORDAN COULD HAVE gone home, but she opted to make breakfast for her and Linc instead. While he showered, which she'd already done, she headed to the kitchen.

Going through his cupboards, she found everything she needed to make French toast. Not because he went food shopping or cooked for himself but because someone did it for him. Mrs. Farley made certain his fridge and cabinets were stocked. She cooked dinner for him if he was going to be home and left it for him to heat.

Which meant, Jordan thought as she flipped the bread in the frying pan, she was spoiling him more. But she didn't mind. As usual, he'd been there for her and pressed her to deal with something she'd have otherwise buried deep. She couldn't help but be grateful for last night and this morning even if she was setting herself up for heartbreak each time she gave in and found herself in his bed.

In her heart, she knew Linc would never intentionally hurt her. She'd also discovered she couldn't resist him. All she could do was to move forward and do her best not to let this happen again. But she wasn't going to beat herself up for being with him, either.

Her body hurt in the best ways. Muscles were sore, reminding her of how good they'd been together. How in sync. How well he read her need.

Her cell phone rang from its place on the granite countertop, *Mom* showing up on the screen. She winced because she'd owed her mother a phone call for too long. They normally spoke more often, but Jordan had been so busy since coming home from Florida, she hadn't had a chance to do more than exchange texts with her parent. She didn't want to talk to her now, from Linc's, but at this point, her mother would worry if Jordan didn't take the call.

She picked up the phone and touched the accept button. "Hi, Mom." She tucked the phone between her ear and shoulder.

"Jordan Marie, where have you been? I called you a few times last night and again this morning."

She cringed. She'd never wanted to worry her mother. "I'm fine, Mom. Sorry. It's been a little crazy." She added a slice of toast from the frying pan to the plate where the other finished pieces were before placing the final coated piece onto the pan.

"Is Linc working you that hard?" her mother asked.

"No, Mom. His new sister had a baby last night."

"Oh, a baby! A boy or a girl?" her mom asked.

Jordan smiled. "A girl. Unnamed but I'm sure Aurora will pick one soon. And the baby is the sweetest thing."

"You were there? At the hospital?" Her mom sounded surprised.

"Yes. Actually I was in the room with Aurora when she gave birth." As Jordan spoke, she braced herself for a negative reaction.

"I don't understand. Wasn't there someone from the family who could have been with her? You aren't family."

Ouch. "I'm well aware. And if I wasn't, you certainly remind me of it often enough," she snapped.

Her mother sighed. "Honey, I'm not trying to be mean. I'm just reminding you of your place. One day the man you call your best friend is going to find a woman to marry, and where will that leave you?"

Jordan flipped the bread and did her best to

breathe and not let her mother's words get to her, but it was hard after spending the night in Linc's bed, sleeping in his arms.

"Can we talk about something else?" she asked.

"Sure. Did I tell you the fire alarm went off in my building the other night? We all had to go outside, and I was wearing my robe…" Her mother went on with her story, and Jordan murmured the requisite *mmm-hmms* while she spoke.

By the time she hung up, her good mood had been ruined by her mother's judgmental assessment of her place in Linc and Aurora's life. It only served to reinforce all the negative thoughts Jordan already held about why they could never be together long-term and why she needed to be better about guarding her heart.

Chapter Eight

"JORDAN, HOLD MY calls," Linc said as he exited his office. "I'll be holed up in the conference room with Brian. No interruptions."

"Got it!" She turned her attention back to work.

In the two weeks since she'd slept with Linc again, they'd fallen back into their normal routine, working during the day, occasional dinners together, and yes, he'd taken her to Ocean Prime for lunch as promised, but he'd been a total gentleman. She had a hunch he was letting her deal with her feelings and come to the conclusion he wanted. That they made sense together, at least sexually. Or maybe he was willing to go back to being her best friend. Whatever the reason, she was concentrating on the present.

This weekend was the baby shower Chloe had planned at the country club the Kingston family belonged to. Jordan had never been comfortable at the club during the times she'd been invited to events there, but thankfully she didn't have to attend often. She wasn't intimidated by the clothing, handbags, and shoes the women there owned, but they made sure to let her know her designer choices weren't up to their standards. If not with words, then with a sneer or a distinct way of looking her over and finding her lacking. Especially the women in Linc's family's social circle.

Although this was a party in a separate room, the rest of the club was open to members, so Jordan was prepared to run into the women who resented her friendship with Linc and always had.

After a morning of work, Jordan decided to eat at her desk today. She wasn't in the mood to go out. Linc was still meeting in the conference room with Brian and a private investigator who he'd hired to look for Wallace. The man was still missing.

Linc also had upcoming meetings with banks and lenders to cover the money needed for the deal with Beck. Anything not to lose a portion of his beloved company to the man he had long-standing issues with.

She walked to the kitchen, pausing to say hello to Suzanne and some of the other women who worked in the office. After taking her yogurt out of the refrigerator, she returned to her desk to find a female with long jet-black hair and a fitted dress tapping her foot impatiently in front of Jordan's desk.

As she drew closer and she saw the woman's profile, Jordan recognized the visitor. Angelica Winston, Linc's ex. One Jordan had never gotten along with, not for lack of trying on her part.

Jordan strode around her desk before acknowledging the clearly impatient woman. "Angelica."

"Jordan. I've been waiting," she said, pursing her red lips in annoyance.

Settling into her seat and placing her lunch on the desk, she met the woman's gaze. "I wasn't aware you had an appointment."

She straightened her shoulders. "I shouldn't need one. I knocked on his door but he didn't answer. Just let him know I'm here," she said.

"Please would be nice," Jordan muttered. "Linc is in a meeting, and I have no idea when he'll be out." Ignoring the woman, Jordan opened her yogurt container and picked up her spoon.

Angelica cleared her throat. "Again, if you would do your job and tell him I'm here, I know he'll come out to talk to me."

As she spoke, Linc approached his office from behind her. "Angelica, what are you doing here?" Linc asked, sounding tired from the day he'd already had.

"Linc, I missed you and I wanted to talk. She wouldn't let you know I was here."

The woman ought to consider herself fortunate, because without him there, Jordan would have ripped into her about how she wouldn't do a damn thing for someone so rude.

"Because I told her I didn't want to be interrupted by anyone." He shot Jordan a grateful look, which Angelica caught.

Unfortunately the woman didn't take a hint. "I'm not just anyone. Now that you're here, we need to talk." She hooked her arm in his and directed him around Jordan's desk and to his office. Short of shaking her off, he had no choice but to deal with her.

Maybe Jordan ought to feel bad for him, but he'd chosen to get involved with a stage-five clinger. What did he expect?

He opened the door to his office, and Angelica pushed them inside. Jordan couldn't help but watch, and as she attempted to shut the door, Linc flung it open again, making his point.

Despite Angelica's proprietary action, Jordan knew he hadn't been involved with the woman for a long time, but they had been in an on-again, off-again relationship, and based on his past behavior, Angelica had every right to think she could talk him into another go-round.

"Angelica, stop. No. We need to talk." Linc sounded pissed.

Jordan cringed at the thought of her touching him, admitting jealousy had crept up on her the minute Linc was alone with the bitch.

"But Linc, it's been so long. Neither one of us is

involved with anyone and we're good together." Her nasal whine grated on Jordan's nerves.

She hated blatantly eavesdropping on what should be a private conversation, but he'd deliberately opened the door. And Jordan wanted to hear what he'd say to the part about him not being involved with anyone.

Though they hadn't touched each other in two weeks, the possessive streak she hadn't known about reared its ugly head. About a man she was trying not to get more attached to.

"You don't know anything about my private life," Linc said.

"I know more than you think. Your mother had lunch with mine, and she was bemoaning her oldest son still being single. Chloe's getting married and she's younger than you. Isn't it time you started thinking about settling down?"

Jordan pushed aside the yogurt she'd been about to eat, her stomach suddenly churning.

"Not with you. Angelica, listen. You're right. We had a good run when neither of us was involved with anyone else, but that's all it was. Two people scratching an itch."

Jordan winced. Oh, he did not say that to her. Talk about a typically dense man.

"Lincoln!" Angelica wailed. "You can't mean that. I was giving you space and time to get other women out of your system. I was waiting for you to come around."

"I'm sorry. Really. But I never led you on. Never told you we had a future." Linc lowered his voice, compassion in his tone.

"Who is she?" Angelica asked loudly, not caring if she caused a scene at his office.

"Who?" Linc asked.

"If it's not me you have a future with, then who is it?"

Linc's groan was a mix of annoyance and frustration. Jordan recognized it well. "No one you need to concern yourself with."

He hadn't mentioned Jordan by name, but he didn't deny there was someone, either.

"Come. I'll walk you out," Linc said.

"Don't touch me. You led me on. I was waiting for you." Angelica's voice sounded closer to the door.

"I never gave you any reason to think you should."

Jordan spun her chair around, picked up her spoon, and managed to eat a spoonful, swiping her mouse to turn on her computer screen and look busy.

Angelica's heels sounded, and she came storming out of the office and past Jordan's desk, striding through the office, an angry woman who didn't care if anyone else knew it.

Wincing, Jordan focused on her lunch, wondering

if Linc would come out of his office, whether or not he realized she'd heard it all, and unsure of what she'd say if he did.

Instead he shut the door and remained inside for the rest of the afternoon.

LINC LEANED AGAINST the office door and let out a groan. Jesus Christ. He hadn't led Angelica on, nor had he given her any indication there would be a future between them. With everything hanging over his head with the business, the last thing he needed was female drama. Another reason he appreciated Jordan. She didn't do drama. She never had.

Speaking of Jordan, he cringed at the realization she'd overheard his conversation. He wasn't ready to face her, so he settled in behind his desk to work, but he was distracted by his missing CFO and his need to borrow way too much money for his liking.

When a knock sounded on his door, he was grateful for the distraction. "Come in!"

His sister bounced into the room, obviously in a good mood. Her cheery smile matched her bright pink dress.

"Hey, Chloe."

She smiled wide. "Hi!" She shut the door behind her and sat down in a chair across from him. "Good time? Bad time?"

"For you? Always a good time." He let go of his stress and focused on his sister. Rising, he walked around the desk and sat on the edge. "How's the baby shower planning going?"

Though Aurora had had the baby early, Chloe was going ahead with the shower since it was as much of a way to introduce Aurora as family as it was to celebrate the baby she'd named Leah.

"Great. I have Faith Dare doing the specialty desserts," she said of Jason Dare's wife.

Linc had stayed in touch with Braden and Willow, keeping them up to date on Aurora and how she was fitting in here. The Prescotts, it turned out, were part of the interesting Dare family, something he'd learned from Chloe. She'd been curious about the people who'd taken her sister in, then she'd been fascinated by the Dare family tree. Faith was married to Jason Dare, a cousin of Austin's who lived in New York.

From there Chloe had discovered Faith's Sweet Treats in the city, and with Willow and Braden coming to the baby shower, Chloe had obviously decided to bring Braden's family into the mix.

"Sounds like you have everything under control," he said, glad she was enjoying the preparation.

She nodded. "I definitely do," she said, suddenly squirming in her seat, a habit left over from when she was a child.

Chloe had a tell and couldn't lie worth a damn. "Okay, spill it," Linc said. "What else is on your mind?"

She sighed. "I didn't want to ask you this sooner because it felt wrong, what with Dad's surprise passing and it feeling so soon." She swallowed hard, clearly struggling.

Of all the siblings, Linc knew their father best because they'd worked together, but they hadn't been close. And Kenneth hadn't understood his writer or rock star sons. Chloe had looked up to him because he was their father, but as soon as she was old enough to catch on to their mother's misery, she'd shut their father out, too.

"It's okay. Whatever it is, you can say it." Linc didn't want her to feel she couldn't come to him.

Twisting her hands in front of her, she forced herself to speak. "Dad was going to walk me down the aisle because it was tradition. But I'm closer to you anyway and now he's gone." She glanced up, her eyes watery. "Linc, will you walk me down the aisle?"

He smiled at his baby sister, who was clearly no longer a baby. Although he didn't think Owen was good enough for her, the wedding was set, and Linc wanted her to be happy. "Of course I will."

"Thank you!" She popped up from her chair and

hugged him, nearly knocking him over in her exuberance.

"Did you think I'd say no?" he asked as she stood up so he could catch his balance.

"No." She shook her head. "But I know how you feel about Owen." Looking up at him with those familiar blue eyes, she all but dared him to say something negative about her fiancé.

He drew a deep breath and took a moment to phrase things so she didn't get hurt. "I just want the right man for you," he said.

"And Owen is that man. We have a lot of things in common. He makes me feel safe, and unlike Dad, he's a good man who won't cheat."

Chloe seemed so damned certain and sincere, but Linc wasn't sure. If she was marrying the man for safety's sake, the tax attorney might fit the bill, but his vibrant sister needed so much more. He hoped she wasn't making a mistake.

Still, he schooled his features and forced a smile. "If you're happy, then I'm glad."

Her shoulders dropped and she relaxed. "So who's your plus-one for the wedding?" she asked as he lowered himself into his chair.

What a day to ask him when he was still reeling over Angelica's unexpected visit. "I'll be coming with Jordan."

His sister rolled her eyes. "Of course Jordan is coming. She's invited but who's your date?"

He looked his sister in the eye and repeated his answer. "Jordan."

Her eyes opened wide. "You and Jordan?" She shook her head as if she'd misunderstood. "Oh, I get it. You want to fend off all the single ladies. That makes sense. Smart, Linc. Very smart." She laughed until she saw he was deadly serious. "Whoa. Wait. You and Jordan?" she asked again. "Does she know she's your date?"

It was Linc's turn to chuckle. "No, actually, she doesn't."

"Linc!"

"She doesn't know she's my date to Aurora's shower either." He shrugged but he had no plans to explain things to his sister. "I'd appreciate it if you'd let me work things out my own way."

Chloe nodded. With one hand, she raised her fingers to her mouth and gestured that her lips were sealed.

"Good to know."

"Okay, I need to get back to work. Behave yourself, Linc. I have a feeling you're in over your head." Chloe braced her hands on the desk and leaned in. "Jordan isn't one of us. Not like you think."

Narrowing his gaze, he asked, "What in the hell do

you mean?"

"Listen." Chloe sat back down in the chair, and he sensed a lecture coming on. "You and Jordan are best friends and always have been, but you're a guy. And you don't see what girls do. The way women in your social circle look at her because her mother was our maid. Jordan has access to you, and people in our world resent her."

"Again, you mean other women resent her."

Chloe nodded. "Jordan might dress in designer clothes, and she knows how to hold herself and behave at the club, but nobody sees her as anything other than the help's daughter."

Anger filled him at the truth of her statement. "What kind of bullshit is this *our world?*" he asked with quotes around the words.

Sure, her mother and his father believed they shouldn't even be friends, but he'd had no idea there were more people who bought into the antiquated notion.

Chloe glanced down, her cheeks flushed. "It's something insecure bitches use to distinguish themselves from smart, beautiful women like Jordan who make their own way in the world and do it well."

At least his sister didn't buy into social class distinctions. What a load of crap, and Linc ground his teeth in frustration.

"Jordan's mother feels the same way. She's always telling her she doesn't belong with me. Not even as my friend."

Chloe's expression turned sad. "What about you? If you had to walk into a charity event or the club with Jordan on your arm, knowing what people would think and say, how would you feel?"

"Proud." He knew the answer without thinking.

His sister's smile was all the validation he needed. "Then go for it and I'll be right by your side." She came around and hugged him again. "Love you, Linc."

"Love you back. Now go work."

Chloe walked out and Linc glanced around his office. Chloe had given him a lot to think about when it came to Jordan. So much more made sense to him now. The morning after they'd last been together, he'd walked into the kitchen as she'd been hanging up the phone after a call from her mother.

He'd sensed immediately things had changed. As usual, Tamara had probably filled her head with her negative feelings about their relationship. If Tamara knew he was sleeping with her daughter, she would lose her mind. And Jordan knew it.

On top of that, according to Chloe, Jordan also felt she didn't fit in. He shook his head at the thought. As if money made a person a decent human being. Jordan was worth ten times more than a dense, shallow woman like Angelica. So was Chloe. Money had nothing to do with it.

One thing was certain, Linc didn't care what anyone thought.

Now how to convince Jordan?

JORDAN PACKED HER things up for the day. She hadn't had a minute alone with Linc. He'd had back-to-back visitors throughout the afternoon, which wasn't unusual. At the moment, he was on the phone with a potential lender, so she left him a text on his phone letting him know she was leaving and she would see him in the morning.

She headed out and decided to take the subway instead of an Uber or company car, needing the fresh air she'd get as she walked the three blocks to the station. She'd been light-headed this afternoon and a little queasy and had attributed it to only eating half her yogurt for lunch. After listening to Angelica's play for Linc, she hadn't felt like eating.

Knowing she was too tired to prep food, she stopped at the grocery store near her apartment and picked up a couple of precooked meals before going home. At least she'd have them for the week. Once home, she put the meals in the fridge and changed into a pair of soft sweats and the tee shirt she'd stolen from

Linc. Nobody had to know she slept in it whenever it didn't need to be washed.

She microwaved and ate the pasta she'd bought and settled herself into her couch, suddenly tired. When her cell rang, it woke her, and a glance at the phone told her she'd fallen asleep for over an hour.

She answered the call, which was her doorman. "Hello?"

"Good evening, Miss Greene. Mr. Kingston is here."

She really should put him on her permanent list, but she liked the heads-up before anyone came over. It gave her a few minutes to … whatever. Clean up. Look in the mirror. "Send him up, please. Thank you."

Knowing she didn't have much time, she chose the look-in-the-mirror option, saw the sleep line on her cheek, and groaned. Just wonderful.

She ran her fingers through her tangled hair and couldn't do much more before he knocked on her door. She wasn't surprised he'd shown up. Not after the scene with his ex.

She let him in and shut the door behind him.

"We need to talk," he said without saying hello first.

She smiled grimly. "If it's about Angelica, I can live without the details."

"But I need you to know a few things." He

shrugged off his jacket and laid it over a club chair, making himself at home.

She sighed as he pulled on his tie, releasing the knot and unthreading the ends. He tossed it over his jacket and proceeded to undo the top two buttons on his shirt and roll up his sleeves.

Dammit, why did he have to be so sexy?

"Are you hungry? I picked up a couple of dinners on my way home."

He shook his head. "I grabbed something first. You don't need to feed me," he said, his lips lifting in a wry grin.

"So you had a busy day." No point beating around the bush, she thought, striding over to her favorite corner of her couch before he could beat her to it.

He settled in right beside her, half facing her, his knee on the couch, touching her thigh.

"Yes, I did. And I want you to know I haven't been with her in over a year. Frankly I hadn't been with anyone, because I've been over having meaningless sex. Angelica called the night I showed up at your apartment drunk. I was on my way over and I made it clear I wasn't interested. Obviously she needed me to be harsher than I was, because she didn't buy it."

Jordan had to admit she was relieved to hear there hadn't been anyone else in a while.

"I know she's a stage-five clinger." It really was her

favorite expression, Jordan mused.

He tipped his head back and laughed. "Great description."

"It does fit."

"Chloe's excited about the baby shower this weekend," he said.

Jordan smiled. "So is Aurora. She's nervous about meeting so many strangers, but she's looking forward to it, too."

His warm gaze met hers. "Do you talk to her often?"

"Every day, every other day, depends. I check in or she calls. She's a wonderful girl given all she had to live through. She hasn't been hardened by life, and she's open to her new family. It's been great to see."

He stretched an arm over the back of the sofa, his fingers running over the skin on her shoulder. A light touch but her entire body tingled, awareness shooting through her veins and her nipples puckering beneath her cotton tee shirt.

"So about the party," Linc said. "It starts at eleven a.m. I'll pick you up around ten."

"Can you fit the huge horse rocker you bought into the back of your SUV?" she asked, grinning. He was such a sucker for buying Aurora and the baby things and having them delivered to the house.

"I already had Max drop it off at the club. Does

ten work for you?"

She nodded. "Perfect. I appreciate the ride." Otherwise she'd have to take an Uber and that wouldn't be fun at all.

"Jordan."

At the gruff sound of his voice, she jerked her head up. "What?"

"You don't thank your date for picking you up to go somewhere." He gripped her arm in his hand, firmly but without hurting her. "Make no mistake. You're my date."

She opened her mouth to argue. To tell him they couldn't show up and act like a couple in front of his family when nobody had any idea they were dating, let alone had any kind of intimate relationship. Not to mention, they hadn't had a discussion laying out the parameters of said relationship.

But she couldn't deny they were involved in a deeper way than they'd been before they'd slept together the first time.

"Linc, we don't want to give your family the wrong impression."

His father would roll over in his grave if he walked into the country club with her on his arm. She had no idea what his mother would say. And though Jordan could handle whatever people dished out, she didn't want to embarrass his family during a day that belonged to Aurora.

"You're right. And we won't." He rose to his feet, leaned over, and pressed his mouth to hers, parting her lips and sucking on her tongue.

She moaned and kissed him back, unable to resist him even when he was his pushy self. By the time he pulled back, she would have agreed to almost anything he'd asked.

"Good night," he said. "Sweet dreams." He strode past the chair, grabbing his jacket and tie.

She was still lost in that kiss, wrapped up in his masculine scent, and her head spinning when the door shut behind him.

Dammit! He'd played her. He knew she wouldn't argue if he kissed her into submission.

She had to find a way to deal with their new relationship, and she decided here and now it was a temporary thing. She would sleep with him when it suited them, be with him and try to enjoy the time they had, but when it was time to move on, she would let him go. Because their worlds didn't mix, and that wasn't something she could change.

As for the shower, they were both invited, so it wasn't unusual for them to show up together. Or so she convinced herself because she had no other choice.

Chapter Nine

LINC PICKED UP Jordan and drove them to the club near his mother's house. She looked gorgeous in a fitted navy dress gathered at the waist and flared out beneath. Throughout the car ride, he was enveloped by her delicious scent, and arousal wound its way through his veins. If they didn't have a party to go to, he'd put up the privacy divider and slide his hand up her dress and find out what she was wearing underneath.

Instead he looked out the window and attempted to focus on the scenery they passed so when they arrived his cock wasn't tenting his pants and on obvious display.

She made small talk and he did as well. She clearly wanted things to feel normal between them. Since she had a big day ahead of her, dealing with the club atmosphere and his entire family, he decided not to push himself on her beforehand. After was another story.

Finally Max pulled up at the club, and they slid out of the car. "I'll bring the gifts in," his driver said.

Linc pressed his hand behind Jordan's back as they walked up the stairs, and he held the door open as they stepped inside.

"Are you okay?" he couldn't stop himself from asking.

She nodded. "Why wouldn't I be? I know everyone at the party, and your brothers and Chloe always make me feel welcome. Plus I love Aurora. There's no reason to worry about me." Her smile reassured him.

Whatever Chloe thought about Jordan not fitting in, she appeared confident and ready. "Then let's go," he said.

His sister had reserved a private room, and when they entered, the décor stood out. On the tables, pink, silver, and white balloons were tied together, encircled with matching flowers around the base of each centerpiece. White cloths with pink liners covered the tabletops, surrounded by white chairs with huge baby-pink bows.

Jordan saw Aurora across the room and immediately headed in her direction. She hugged his new sister and then turned her attention to Leah, who was snuggled in a car seat carrier. Bending down, Jordan lifted the baby into her arms and held her against her chest, supporting her head with her hand.

It wasn't the first time he'd seen her hold the baby, but in the hospital, he'd been worried about Jordan's emotional state. Right now he was concerned with his own. At the sight of her cradling the infant, his chest felt heavy, and a lump settled in his throat, while a panicky feeling took hold.

He'd definitely had issues with the notion of having kids, thanks to his father's behavior and how it had impacted what he and his siblings had seen and heard growing up.

"What are you staring at?" Xander asked, walking up beside him and cutting off anything else he'd been about to consider.

Linc glanced at his brother. "Nothing. How have you been?"

Xander shot him a curious glance. "What's going on?"

Linc shook his head, not about to get into a conversation about feelings even he didn't understand. And not at a place where someone could overhear.

"I'm good. Talking to the studio about the filming of my next project." He shrugged. "Hanging in. You?"

Linc groaned. "Busy at work. Dad left some issues that have recently come to light. Wrapping up those loose ends hasn't been easy."

"Son of a bitch," Xander muttered. "Sorry to hear that."

"I'll get it sorted." Linc glanced around the room, taking in his mom and Chloe, who both caught his gaze and waved from where they were talking to their friends.

Chloe had invited people her age, and his mom had included her acquaintances, giving Aurora an opportunity to meet a lot of people at once.

"I'm really proud of Mom," Linc said. "What other woman would take her husband's illegitimate child in and treat her like her own?"

Xander shook his head. "None that I know of. Just another reason Dad was an ass."

"I'm here! We can start the party!"

Linc looked toward the front of the room, where the familiar voice had come from, to find Dash standing in the doorway, a grin on his face. Making an entrance, as usual.

Linc shot Xander an amused grin, and they headed over to greet their brother. When he got busy working, not even a bomb going off could interrupt Dash's creative process. Although his mother had told Linc that Dash had come by to meet Aurora and Linc was glad.

"Hey!" Dash said, coming up and pulling first Xander, then Linc into a one-armed hug.

"Look who dressed up for the occasion." Xander patted Dash on the back of his partially unbuttoned white collared dress shirt.

His sleeves were rolled up, revealing his tattooed

arms. Linc enjoyed his brother's different style, the opposite of his own conservative attire. Including the tight black jeans, unripped thanks to club rules, and black Nike Air Jordans.

"Tell me you missed me," Dash said, laughing.

"Go away. Say hello to your mother," Linc muttered.

Ignoring the stares all the women shot his way, Dash made his way across the room and hugged first their mom and then Aurora and Jordan before turning his attention to the baby.

Family, Linc thought. His meant everything to him.

JORDAN SAT NEXT to Linc at a table with Xander, Dash, Chloe, Melly, and Aurora, the family closing ranks and making a statement for their new sister and her baby. Also joining them were Braden Prescott and Willow James, who'd remained close with Aurora. The couple had gotten engaged at the last dinner they'd all enjoyed together in Miami and were clearly happy now.

Aurora had been brought to tears more than once during the lavish day, and Melly had introduced the young girl to all of her friends, who'd fawned over the baby and brought very expensive gifts.

Jordan had been on the receiving end of various looks, mostly from Chloe's friends. The women in Melly's age bracket tended to ignore her, but the women closer to her own age? They'd either scanned her from head to toe, cataloging her clothing and appearance, turning up their noses and glancing away, or shot her annoyed glances.

Jordan had no doubt they resented her position next to Linc. She'd overheard more than one group of women discussing his lack of a girlfriend and potential availability, despite Jordan sitting beside him, his hand occasionally brushing her shoulder or twirling her hair. Even when she'd tried to inch her chair away.

Aurora had raised an eyebrow at what she'd seen and grinned widely. Melly had been too busy to notice, but Jordan's stomach had been in knots worrying about upsetting his mother on such a special day. Who knew how she would react? She was fine with Jordan being a friend of the family, but she couldn't imagine Melly would approve of the maid's daughter being involved with her oldest son.

Despite her nerves, Jordan had enjoyed Aurora's baby shower, probably more than her brothers had, considering all the baby games Chloe had arranged for everyone to play. Traditionally men were not invited to a shower, but with this also being Aurora's introduction to their friends, Chloe hadn't adhered to custom.

When she'd handed out baby pins and made everyone pin one on their shirt, including the men, Jordan nearly choked at the look on Linc's face. Chloe had then instructed everyone not to say the word *baby*. If anyone heard another person utter the word, they could take that person's pin. The person with the most pins won a prize.

Jordan had to admit it was endearing watching the Kingston brothers endure games from Don't Say Baby to Dirty Diapers, in which a variety of candy bars were placed in newborn-sized diapers and people had to guess what kind of candy they were eating. Even Jordan had nearly gagged at the idea, shocking herself at how nauseous she'd become.

By the time food was served and Faith Dare's cake pops brought out to each table, Jordan was exhausted. For a woman who worked eight- to ten-hour days, she was surprised a party had wiped her out so badly. She also needed to use the ladies' room.

Glancing at Linc, she said, "I'll be back in a few minutes."

He nodded, standing as she did and pulling out her chair. Such a gentleman, she mused.

As she rose, Aurora stood up as well. "I'll go with you," she said and turned to Willow. "Will you watch Leah?" The baby had been sleeping quietly in her car seat in the chair next to Aurora.

"Of course." Willow smiled and put a hand on the back of the chair where the baby slept.

Jordan followed Aurora out of the room, then pointed her in the direction of the ladies' room. She passed the main dining room, where normal lunch activities were going on, and the loud chatter sounded as they walked by.

Once inside, she and Aurora closed themselves in their own stalls. Jordan was quick, then washed her hands before heading to the outer sitting area. She placed her bag on a shelf below a wall-to-wall mirror and pulled out her lip gloss.

Glancing in the mirror, she was shocked by how pale she appeared. She didn't have blush with her, so she had no way to put life back in her cheeks. With a sigh, she opened the gloss stick and applied it to her lips, as the sound of women's voices and laughter alerted her to incoming women.

They entered, continuing to talk to one another, and Jordan grasped her purse and stepped aside to wait for Aurora.

"Jordan?"

She turned at the sound of her name and forced herself not to visibly cringe. "Angelica. Hi."

"I take it you're here for Linc's new sister's baby shower. My mother is there, too." Her fake smile grated on Jordan's nerves.

"Yes, I saw your mother." Carol Winston was a good friend of Melly's. They all ran in the same social circles.

Angelica's friends disappeared into the other room, and Aurora had walked in, standing behind Jordan.

Jordan had no intention of introducing them. "Well, it was nice to see you, but I need to get back inside." Jordan turned toward Aurora, but Angelica tapped her shoulder and Jordan spun back around. "Yes?"

"Since we're both here, I thought I'd give you some advice. You know, woman to woman?" Angelica said, fake kindness oozing from her voice as she twirled a long strand of her black hair around a finger.

Oh, this ought to be good, Jordan thought. "Aurora, why don't you go ahead, and I'll meet you back inside."

"That's okay. I'll wait." She stepped up to Jordan's side.

Angelica looked at her but didn't spare her a thought, her gaze zeroing in on Jordan. "You're not his type. You know that, right?"

"Whose type?" Jordan opted for playing dumb. Let this bitch spell it out for her.

"Linc. Everyone knows you want him. It's been obvious since you were a kid and your mother was cleaning his house. I looked into the party room and saw his hand on your shoulder, touching your hair. When no one was looking, of course."

Jordan kept her face blank and let Angelica spew her venom.

Her face had contorted into an ugly expression, revealing who she really was inside. "But let's face it. If he's sleeping with you, it's temporary. You don't belong in his life. You can't fit in like I can. And as soon as he realizes that, he'll come back to me."

Jordan's cheeks burned, but she otherwise refused to let Angelica see she'd hit a nerve. "Are you really sure? Because according to Linc, he was never with you in any way that mattered." Turning, she looked at Aurora. "Let's go."

Aurora shook her head. "One minute." She walked over to Angelica, who'd begun to reapply her lipstick. "I haven't known my brother long, but I know he's a good man. And he would never be with someone who has a soul as ugly as you do." She glanced at Jordan. "Now I'm ready."

Together they walked out of the ladies' room. Jordan's insides were trembling. She didn't like confrontation, but she wouldn't let anyone treat her like shit. Even if the things Angelica said were the same words her mother had tried to teach her. Words she was being force-fed from all sides, it seemed. Even from herself.

"You didn't have to stand up for me, but I appreciate that you did," Jordan said.

"I grew up in foster care. I learned how to stand up for myself and the few people I cared about." Aurora met her gaze. "You know she's wrong. You and Linc are perfect for each other."

Jordan grasped her hand. "I know you care and I am so grateful. I care about you, too. As far as Angelica, she might have been hateful when she said it, but she wasn't far off base. These people look at me and see the maid's daughter."

"But Linc doesn't see that! And if you don't fit in with them, then I don't either," Aurora said, her tone adamant.

Jordan smiled at the young woman who was special in her own right. "Yes, you do belong. You're part of their family and don't you ever forget it." She squeezed Aurora's hand tight and released her grasp. "Come on. Let's get back before people wonder what happened to us."

They returned to the party to find Willow holding the baby, who needed to be fed. Aurora hurried to her daughter, and Jordan sat back down beside Linc, feeling numb after the confrontation she hadn't asked for or wanted.

In what day and age did people talk about class as if where you came from mattered? She didn't understand it, and she resented everyone in this room who tried to make her feel less than. Her parents had worked hard to give her a good life, and Jordan wasn't the least bit ashamed of their jobs or who they were. In their hearts, they were better people than anyone who'd looked down on her today.

"Are you okay? You look pale." Linc caressed her cheek, and she did her best not to lean into his touch the way she wanted to.

She nodded. "I haven't been feeling great the last couple of days. I think I'm just tired."

Concern etched his handsome features. "Why don't you take some time off. A few days until you're one hundred percent."

"Thank you but I'm sure I'm fine."

"Well, if you wake up and you don't feel great, stay home."

She nodded.

Aurora returned after feeding the baby and walked over to Jordan and Linc's side of the table. "Did Jordan tell you about the bitch in the bathroom?"

Jordan flinched. She should have told Aurora not to say anything, but it hadn't even occurred to her.

Linc's eyes narrowed. "What is she talking about? What happened?"

Aurora, who was holding Leah against her shoulder and patting the baby's back, looked from Linc to

Jordan, understanding filling her gaze. "Oops! I need to go sit down. It's easier to burp her when I'm sitting," she rattled, then turned and walked back to her chair.

"Jordan?"

"It was no big deal. Just a run-in with Angelica. Nothing I can't handle." She'd thought that was true, but then why was she trembling inside? Why was a lump forming in her throat? And why was she nauseous again?

"Dammit. What did she say to you?" He looked furious, his eyes turning a deep blue, color highlighting his cheekbones.

She forced in a breath of air. "Listen, there are things women say to each other when they're…" She trailed off. There wasn't anything she could come up with to placate him. "It doesn't matter. I handled it."

His body vibrated with anger. "But you shouldn't have to handle her at all."

"I'm wiped out. I'm going to call a car to take me home. You stay with your family for the end of the party. Okay?" Her fingers shook as she picked up her purse and searched for her phone.

He put a hand on her trembling one. "I can leave. It's practically over anyway. At least those horrific games are."

That made her laugh. "I don't want to take you

away from the party or your family."

"My decision. Let's say our goodbyes. Everyone will understand."

Because she knew she couldn't win, she gave in. They made their rounds of thank-yous and goodbyes. Aurora promised to text pictures of the presents she hadn't yet opened and share them later.

And though, when they reached her apartment, Linc wanted to come upstairs and make sure she was okay, she insisted she wanted to fall into bed and go to sleep. Despite his concern, he gave in.

But he didn't look happy about it.

BACK IN HIS apartment after the party, Linc poured himself a glass of Macallan 18 and settled into a chair in the living room, kicking his feet up on the leather ottoman in front of him. He lifted his glass, studying the amber-colored liquid. Today had been … interesting. A baby shower wasn't an event he'd like to repeat, but watching Aurora's face as she took in the room, the stack of presents, and the number of people who'd come was worth sitting through the torture.

He didn't know what she wanted to do with her life, but it was way too soon to ask or pressure her in any way. The conversation would come in time.

His thoughts turned to Jordan and today's mess,

courtesy of Angelica. It wasn't like Chloe hadn't warned him about the women at the club and in their family's world, but it had been hard for him to comprehend. Until Jordan had been exposed to Angelica's venom firsthand. Linc had no idea what his ex had said, but Jordan had obviously been shaken, and Aurora hadn't liked it either. He wanted to know but Jordan wouldn't talk. Hell, she hadn't even wanted him around. Giving her space seemed like a good idea, but if she didn't eventually tell him, he wasn't above asking Aurora for details.

With that settled, he turned his thoughts to the business. Despite how much the company was currently leveraged, Linc had borrowed the money to pay Beck from a trusted lender. Next week, Linc would meet with the man to hand him a check and have the satisfaction of seeing his face when Linc informed him he wouldn't get his hands on any part of Kingston Enterprises. Linc would have no choice but to be a partner in this deal, but he'd keep Beck away from the family business.

Based on his calculations, Linc could fix things over the next five years, and he took solace in knowing he had a plan. His father's surprise investments kept coming to light, but he thought they'd uncovered them all now. Linc would set things right. But he still needed to find Wallace and find out exactly how his father had gotten them into this situation and why. His dementia was only part of the story, of that Linc was certain.

His phone buzzed, and he pulled his cell from his pocket to see Dash had texted. "We're downstairs and coming up."

We obviously meant Dash and Xander. And because they were on the permanent list downstairs, Linc was lucky they'd given him warning before descending on him and his well-stocked bar.

He rose from his seat and pulled out extra glasses from the cabinet above the counter in the corner of the living room before heading to the door. He opened it just as Dash and Xander exited the elevator.

They strode past him with muttered hellos and entered, heading straight to the bar.

"Make yourselves at home," he said, shutting the door, as they took their bottle of choice and poured themselves a drink.

"Jesus, I need one after the day we endured." Xander slugged back the contents of his glass, and Dash did the same, adding more before settling on the sofa.

Linc refilled his glass and joined them, sitting back in the chair.

"Who the hell came up with the idea of filling diapers with candies that look like shit?" Dash leaned an elbow on the arm of the couch.

Linc shook his head. "Beats me. But Aurora enjoyed it and I'm glad it's over."

His brothers nodded in agreement.

"How are you both doing with Aurora?" Linc asked, wondering if they were getting close with her.

"She's a good kid," Dash said. "But I haven't had much time to get to know her. I'm hoping when I get out of the studio before any touring we'll get together."

Xander nodded. "I've been to the house a few times and we're getting to know each other. I really like her. Life dealt her a shitty hand but she's not bitter. And she's not money hungry despite having access. She impresses me."

Linc leaned back in his seat, comfortable and chilled now that his brothers were here. "How are the songs coming?"

"Depends on the day." Dash shrugged. "It'll come together. It always does."

Linc was so proud of his brothers. Despite their father's lack of interest, they'd both grown up to pursue their dreams. In Xander's case, writing had come after the military, a time Xander didn't like to talk about.

"So what about you? You mentioned you're gearing up for your next movie?" Linc asked him, then lifted his glass and took a sip.

"They're going through casting now. It's been hard

to find the right fit for the part of the wife. They've been screen-testing a shit ton of actresses, but I have faith my producer and director will come through with the perfect woman." Xander sounded certain, so Linc doubted there'd be problems.

"And meanwhile you're writing your next novel?" Dash asked. "Ever consider a rock star as the hero?" He grinned and tossed back the last of his drink.

Xander raised an eyebrow. "No way. My guy is loyal and doesn't fuck his way through every woman he meets. Unlike the rock stars I know."

Dash smirked and let out a laugh. "It's a good life if you can get it. Okay, enough about us. What's going on with you?" He zeroed in on Linc with his penetrating stare.

Knowing he couldn't avoid this forever, he filled his brothers in on what their father had been up to prior to his death and the way he'd handled things.

"Jesus. I'm sorry. If there's anything I can do, let me know." Xander frowned. "I'm shocked he'd make decisions that could hurt the business knowing he had dementia," Xander said.

Linc drew in a long breath. "Well, we do know he never wanted to face his diagnosis. And if he thought he was making good choices, he wasn't worrying about his diminished mental capacity."

"What does Wallace have to do with it? He's supposed to be Dad's good friend." Dash rose from his seat. "Anyone want another?"

Linc and Xander shook their heads, and Dash headed to pour himself more then returned and sat back down on the couch.

"According to his doctor, who I've spoken to, Dad's behavior isn't surprising. As for Wallace, I have a PI tracking him down. I want answers."

His brothers nodded in agreement. They spent the next hour talking, reminiscing, and having a good time, something they didn't get to do together often enough. Everyone's schedules kept them busy.

"So I have a question." Dash looked directly at Linc. "I noticed not only did you show up with Jordan but you had your hands all over her. So to speak. What is up with you two?"

"Now I do need a drink." Linc stood, walked to the bar, and poured himself another scotch before turning back to his brothers. "We slept together. A couple of times."

"I knew it." Xander's tone was the equivalent of a pat on the back. "You finally gave in."

"Yeah. I finally gave in. And so did she."

Dash laughed. "I should have figured out you two would end up together years ago."

Linc raised an eyebrow. "What makes you think it's something permanent?" He couldn't even get her to commit to the word *relationship*, let alone something long-term.

"Well, if any one of us was going to settle down, excluding Chloe, it'd be you. You're the stable one. The one who worries about the rest of us more like a parent," Dash said.

"Because we didn't have a father who gave a shit," Xander helpfully added. "Besides, I saw how you looked at Jordan holding Aurora's baby."

Linc froze. "What?"

"You were mesmerized by the sight, and I actually thought, he's next." Xander grinned, pleased with his observation.

Dash's head swung back and forth between them, the conversation clearly fascinating for him.

Not so much for Linc and he swallowed hard. Yes, he'd reacted to seeing Jordan with the infant, and he'd been shocked by the heavy feeling in his chest. "I have … complicated feelings about kids."

Xander raised his eyebrows. "Yeah? Why?"

"You grew up in our house. Heard Mom crying over Dad. Parents can really screw up a kid's head. Being a father is a lot of responsibility. And I already made sure you three ended up okay," he said wryly.

Dash shot him a grin. "I did my best to make life hard," he said.

"Hanging out in bars when you were sixteen so

you could sing? Yeah, I worried," Linc admitted.

They all might be close in age, but Linc was the oldest and had always felt the burden of responsibility his father hadn't taken on.

Not wanting to continue this discussion, because kids were way ahead of where his head was now, he rose from his seat. "We haven't even figured out how to be together. Jordan's so skittish she might as well be running away. So quit talking about babies," he muttered, and suddenly he was ready for his brothers to go home.

Chapter Ten

L INC ARRIVED AT Beck's place of business and went through the same routine as last time before he was escorted back to talk to him. Although he planned to have the money he owed wired today around the same time as this meeting, Linc wanted one last conversation with the man.

He knocked and walked in, coming face-to-face with his one-time friend. "Beck."

"I was just notified you wired the money." Beck rose from his seat behind the desk. "Guess we're in business."

Linc inclined his head. "Apparently we are. But you didn't succeed in grabbing a part of my company. Despite using an older man's weakness to try and do it." Linc wouldn't come out and admit to his father's illness, but Beck had to have realized something wasn't right when Kenneth Kingston had put up a piece of the family company as collateral in the deal.

Beck shrugged. "You win some, you lose some. But for your information, I had nothing to do with your father's choices."

Not about to let him off the hook easily, Linc stepped toward him. "You could have given me a heads-up and chose not to. You also dragged out the information for your own enjoyment. Can't say I appreciate either choice."

Beck shrugged. "And I can't say I care."

"Great." Linc refrained from rolling his eyes. "With that settled, keep Brian, my CEO, updated on anything having to do with this deal. I don't want to be blindsided again."

Better to let Brian deal with the actual purchase and subsequent renovations and leasing. Linc and Beck might kill one another if they had to work together directly. And since it was Beck who was involved, Linc wouldn't turn it over to someone more junior. To be safe, he wanted someone he trusted implicitly handling it.

"Whatever you say." Beck took his seat again, obviously finished with the conversation, which was fine with Linc.

"Let's try and stay out of each other's orbit from now on," Linc said before turning and walking out, letting the door slam behind him this time.

★　★　★

JORDAN WORKED ALL morning without a break because she'd promised Aurora they could go shopping for post-maternity clothes.

Melly had done so much for her, furnishing the baby's room, supplementing accessories and clothes that she didn't get at the shower. But when it came to her own wardrobe, Aurora wanted someone closer to her own age to join her. Aurora was coming to the office to meet up with Jordan and Chloe for a girls' afternoon.

Jordan had taken off the day after the baby shower, as Linc had offered and she'd returned the next day. For the most part, she was feeling better except for an occasional bout of light-headedness and nausea. She assumed she had a lingering virus, or as a migraine person, she attributed the symptoms to her condition and went about her days.

She looked forward to shopping with the two girls today, and by the time Aurora arrived, Jordan was ready to go.

The young woman walked up to Jordan's desk, an excited smile on her face. "Did you hear the cool news?"

Jordan shook her head. "What's up?"

"Dash and the band are performing at a special charity event this Saturday night and we're all going! Melly asked the nanny her friend's daughter used if she could babysit for Leah and she said yes." She vibrated with excitement and Jordan was thrilled for her.

"That's amazing. I know you'll have fun." Jordan smiled. "Now how about I call Chloe and we get going?"

"You're going, too! I spoke to Linc on the way here, and he said you would both be there." Aurora bounced on the balls of her feet.

"Oh!"

"Sorry," Linc said, as he came up behind his sister. "Everything came together for Dash and the band this morning, but I was tied up with an appointment and didn't get a chance to tell you. But we're going on Saturday night." He walked past her, stopping outside his office door.

What was with this *we* stuff, anyway? "It sounds like a family event to me."

Jordan glanced at Aurora, who was watching them with interest.

"Aurora, honey, why don't you go find Chloe? I'll be with you in a few minutes. I want to talk to your brother." Jordan pushed herself up from her seat.

"Oh. Sure." Aurora spun and headed to the other side of the office where Chloe worked. She'd been here before and had learned who sat where.

Once she was gone, Jordan walked around her desk, put a hand on Linc's back, and prodded him toward his office. Once inside, she shut the door behind them.

"If you wanted alone time, all you had to do was say so," he said with that sexy grin she couldn't resist.

When she'd taken the day off from work, he'd had a nearby delicatessen send chicken soup and sandwiches over for her to eat. He'd wanted to come by, but she needed sleep, not to mention distance, and he'd agreed to let her rest. And on her return, he'd been on his best behavior, not pushing their relationship, and she'd been grateful for the reprieve.

"What's going on?" She set her hands on her hips and cocked her head to one side.

"Tell me you don't want to see The Original Kings in person?"

"Of course I do, but–"

He shrugged. "No buts. We're going. And Jordan? Now that you've had a week to recuperate and you feel better, after the concert, we're going to talk about us. We've danced around what *this* is long enough." He gestured between them.

She drew a deep breath and mentally acknowledged the need for them to have that conversation. The time had come. Her pulling back and giving in only to pull away again was giving them both whiplash.

Maybe what she needed to do was let their relationship happen and run its course, which she believed it would. Probably not for her, because she'd become emotionally invested. In truth, she already was. But she would go into this knowing they didn't have a future, and she'd eventually have to nurse a broken heart.

Still, if she made it clear to him she understood the parameters, sex only, when things ended, they could go back to the way things had been before.

Decision made, she hoped she could handle it. Meeting his gaze, she nodded. "Okay. We'll talk."

He raised his eyebrows, surprise etching his features. "Good."

He looked like he wanted to say more, to ask her questions, but he'd said they'd discuss things on Saturday night, and she wasn't going to do it in the office. "Well, I need to go meet up with Chloe and Aurora. You're okay by yourself this afternoon?" she asked.

He grinned. "I'll be fine. Are you coming back to the office today?" he asked.

"Doubtful. I think we'll be out till after five. Chloe has shopping *plans*." She used a quote gesture with her fingers.

His sister had laid out a day, beginning with lunch and keeping them hopping from store to store.

He laughed at her description. "Got it."

She turned to leave, and he hooked an arm around her waist, pulling her against him and, before she could react, sealing his lips over hers.

She'd missed this and returned the kiss, opening

her mouth for him and letting his tongue swirl inside. He nipped her lower lip and licked the sting, the hint of pain causing her to moan and inch closer. Her sex clenched and need pulsed through her body, making her wish they weren't in the office.

But for a brief moment, she let herself go. She wrapped her arms around him and indulged. The kiss was wet and hot, everything she dreamed about when she thought of Linc. Until a knock sounded on the door.

Before they could fully pull apart, Chloe walked in, Aurora bumping into her as she came to a sudden halt. "Oh, shit. Sorry!" Chloe exclaimed.

Jordan's face flamed and she buried her face in Linc's chest.

"Ever hear of knocking?" Linc's arm wrapped tighter around her.

"It's an office, not a bedroom," Chloe shot back, sister arguing with her brother. "But I am sorry, Jordan."

Jordan pulled herself together and stepped away. "It's fine. We shouldn't have been…" She cut off her explanation and shook her head. "Are you ready to go?" she asked the women.

"We are." Chloe stepped back, and Aurora, who had already inched out of the doorway, waited for them by Jordan's desk.

Jordan glanced at Linc and spoke quietly, so only he could hear. "I know you don't want anyone to think of you behaving like your father. We shouldn't have been making out in the office," she said, taking partial responsibility even though he'd started it.

He strode over and placed his hands on her shoulders. "My father cheated on my mother. I'm with someone I care about. Totally different. Now go have a good time and stop finding reasons to worry."

She nodded, managed a smile, and headed out for the day.

AT LUNCH, CHLOE and Aurora chatted while they ate. Jordan, suddenly dizzy and nauseous, picked at her salad. They'd been talking about the stores they planned on checking out first, but Jordan had tuned them out. The minute the waitress placed the Cobb salad in front of her, bacon bits and the strong smell of cheese had her stomach churning.

"Jordan? Are you okay?" Chloe's voice calling her name caught her attention, and she shook her head to clear her mind. "Yes, sorry. What were you saying?"

Both women looked at her with concern.

"You haven't eaten anything, and you spaced out for most of our conversation," Aurora said. "What's wrong?"

Jordan sighed. "I haven't been feeling great. I think it's a silent migraine." She'd read up on them earlier today, wondering if she needed to make an appointment with a neurologist. Usually her migraines were painful with throbbing in her head. This was different. All the other symptoms without the pain.

"What's a silent migraine?" Chloe asked, taking a sip of her club soda, her engagement ring twinkling as the sun in the window bounced off the large diamond. "I've never heard of one."

"I actually had to look it up myself, but since I get painful migraines and what I've been feeling has similar symptoms, like nausea and light-headedness and a general blah feeling without the head pain, there's a good chance that's all it is." She shrugged and took a small sip of her own club soda, hoping it would help settle her stomach.

Aurora leaned in closer. "Nausea, huh?"

"Yep."

"And you're light-headed?" she repeated.

"Again, yep."

The young woman narrowed her eyes. "Very tired?

Jordan thought about how she'd been feeling. "Well, yes."

Aurora glanced at Chloe, whose eyes opened wide. Something silent had passed between them.

"Do your boobs hurt?" Aurora asked bluntly.

"What?" Jordan asked loudly, caught herself, and moderated her tone. "I'm sorry. What are you asking me?"

Aurora grinned. "Jordan, could you be pregnant?"

Her words caught Jordan mid-swallow, and she swallowed wrong and began to choke on the bubbles in her drink. "What?" She was beginning to sound like a broken record. "Pregnant? I don't think so!"

And how could she even talk about this with Linc's sisters?

Chloe clasped her hands in front of her, looking shaken but not at all upset. "Okay, so based on what I saw at the shower and today, I'm assuming you and Linc are together."

"Yes. And he's your brother and we don't need to talk about it. But I know we always used protection. Now subject closed. End ... of." Jordan sliced her hand through the air.

But the word *pregnant* lingered between them.

And Aurora wasn't finished. "Nothing is one hundred percent." She shot Jordan a knowing gaze. "How long have you two been ... you know?"

Chloe's eyes were wide, but she appeared focused and was listening.

Jordan swallowed hard. "In Florida. And one more time after that," she said, squirming in her seat. Not because she couldn't discuss sex but because these women were too closely related to the man she'd been with.

"So a little over a month ago." Aurora was a persistent thing, something Jordan was discovering.

She nodded. But she couldn't be pregnant now. She'd gone through that experience before, and early on, which was all she'd had, she'd felt fine. No symptoms until she missed a period. Oh God. She thought about when she'd been due and realized she had skipped her period. With everything going on in her life, she hadn't even realized it. She began to sweat, the possibility of being pregnant now running through her mind.

"We passed a pharmacy on the corner. Let's get the check and you can buy a pregnancy test," Chloe said. She wiped her mouth with her napkin and gestured for the server.

Stunned, Jordan nodded, her mind going back to the first time she and Linc had been together. He hadn't intentionally brought condoms but had found one in his Dopp kit. And it had looked old, like it had been there for a long time. Wincing, she pulled out her wallet to pay.

A little while later, Jordan had purchased the pregnancy tests, a few because she needed to be certain, and the three women returned to the restaurant, which was attached to the mall. Nobody else was in the lounge or the room with the stalls.

Chloe and Aurora sat down in chairs in the waiting area while Jordan, panicked and horrified, closed herself in a stall alone, peed on three sticks, and placed them on top of the boxes they'd come in on the floor in front of her.

And she remained in the private stall, wanting to be as alone as possible.

And she waited.

"Any news?" Aurora called out to her.

She glanced down but her phone and the alarms she'd set hadn't gone off. "Not yet!"

She'd bought three different brands. Unfortunately that meant three different time frames before she got all of the results. One minute, three minutes, five minutes.

Nausea filled her, this time thanks to worry and fear. She'd been down this road before, and the last guy had not taken the news well. Linc's father hadn't taken the news well. It was a wealthy man pattern.

She and Linc didn't make sense as a couple, and the rationale for that conclusion hadn't changed. A pregnancy now would be a nightmare. Sure, Linc wanted them to be together, enjoying sex, having fun. He didn't want kids. He'd once told her about his fear of subjecting children to parents who tried marriage but didn't get along, like his had. And Jordan was still certain she didn't fit into his world.

So the tests had to be negative. They just had to be, she thought, closing her eyes and praying hard.

The first alarm went off on her phone. She shut it and glanced down, seeing a dark line. Fuck!

"Well?" Chloe sounded closer.

"Give me a minute!" Jordan breathed in and out, and finally the second one went off.

She knelt down and this time she saw a plus sign. Closing her eyes, she wanted to cry. Not needing the other one, she turned off her last alarm, scooped up the tests, and walked out, tossing them in the trash.

With Chloe and Aurora surrounding her, she washed her hands, stalling before facing them.

Finally she spoke. "I'm pregnant."

Chloe and Aurora stared at her with wide eyes, clearly stunned.

Before they could say a word, Jordan continued. "And you cannot tell anyone. I'll talk to Linc in my own time and in my own way." They'd planned to be alone after the concert. That gave her a couple of days to come to terms with the situation, and she'd have to find the courage to tell him then.

"Promise me," she said, meeting each of Linc's sisters' gazes. Could this be more awkward?

"Yes, of course," Chloe said, biting her lower lip. "Jordan, I don't know what to say. I don't know how you feel. I…" Trailing off, she merely pulled Jordan into a hug.

Once she released her, Aurora did the same.

Then Chloe grasped Jordan's hands. "Linc loves you. Everything is going to be fine."

Jordan forced a smile. Love wasn't a word they'd ever used, and she didn't kid herself about the future. She'd done this before, and nothing had been fine. She didn't anticipate things going any better now.

JORDAN DIDN'T KNOW how she made it through the week, coming in to work every day and hiding the news of her pregnancy from Linc. She was sure fear and panic were written all over her face, but as he was busy with business deals, he didn't seem to notice.

The private investigator had located Wallace, who'd taken a private jet owned by a friend to the Maldives, which lacked an extradition treaty with the United States. He'd jumped through hoops to hide his tracks, but Linc hadn't been interested in how the CFO had accomplished his disappearing act. He wanted to talk to him and understand what had been going on with his father in his final days.

Now Jordan stood in her bedroom, trying to find something to wear to Madison Square Garden for tonight's concert. She took out her favorite pair of tight dark-washed jeans and slid them on, wriggling her lower body as she pulled them over her thighs and tried to button them around her waist.

They'd always been snug, but she still had to convince herself the tightness as she lay down on the bed to button them was normal. And not the result of her pregnancy.

She chose a light blue silk top with a low-cut V-neck and loose sleeves, tucking in the front and letting the back and sides hang over the jeans. A pair of black over-the-knee boots laced up the outer sides completed the outfit.

Standing in front of the full-length mirror behind her door, she took in her appearance, knowing she wouldn't be wearing tight clothes for much longer. Her hair hung long over her shoulders and her makeup was done.

Grabbing her black leather jacket, she was as ready as she'd ever be to deal with telling Linc he was going to be a father. She was so nervous and worked up, she doubted she'd be able to pay attention to the concert.

Linc picked her up with Max driving, as usual. His eyes lit up when he saw her, but she couldn't find comfort in the fact that he found her attractive. Not when so much more was at stake.

Linc was in a good mood as they drove to MSG, and she tried to put everything out of her head until later. On the way, they chatted, making small talk.

"Will Chloe's fiancé be there tonight?" she asked.

Linc frowned. "No. Concerts are too loud for him. Pussy," he muttered under his breath.

She couldn't help but laugh. "I have a question. Would any man be good enough for your sister?"

He leaned back against the seat. "I take the Fifth."

She laughed. Soon they pulled up at the Garden. Linc helped her out and kept an arm secure around her waist as they pushed past the crowds and headed to the private entrance to the VIP suites. The family had backstage passes, and their tickets were for a box high up in the arena. The actual VIP event was scheduled for after the show for a select group of people allowed to hang out with the band, including family and close friends.

Once inside the box, she said hello to everyone, doing her best to avoid Chloe's and Aurora's curious stares. She was actually glad when Linc made his way over to Aurora and hugged her tight. Jordan trusted the young woman not to spill Jordan's secret.

While waiting for the opening act, she walked over to Xander, who had poured himself a drink.

"Hi there," she said.

"Hi, yourself. Can I get you something?" He gestured to the bar.

"Club soda would be great."

He filled a glass with ice and handed her the cup. "So. What's happening in your life?" he asked.

"I think I'd rather know about the life of a famous novelist," she said, deflecting and turning the subject to him.

He shrugged. "Just writing my next book and talking to the director and producer about the next movie."

"He says modestly." She nudged him with her shoulder. "Who'd have thought the Kingston brother who went off to join the marines would end up being a world-famous thriller writer."

His eyes turned darker. "Writing lets me deal with things without actually having to talk about them."

Every sibling had found their own way to deal with Kenneth Kingston's affairs and painful behavior. Xander's had been to get as far away as he could. No one knew what had happened when he was overseas, but when he returned, he became more of a loner who put his emotions on the page.

"Well, I'm proud of you. In fact, I have an entire bookshelf devoted to your books. Someday I expect you to come sign them." She lifted her cup and took a sip of her bubbly drink.

"It would be my pleasure. Invite me over any time." He winked at her, and she laughed, just as Linc joined them, slipping an arm around Jordan's waist.

"What are you trying to get her to invite you to?" he asked Xander.

"Jordan wants me to sign her X. Kingston collection, and I told her I just need an invite." Xander grinned.

"Just make sure I'm there when this Bozo shows up." Linc pulled her closer and his fingers wrapped nearer to her belly.

She jerked away in panic. "I think I hear the opening act." She turned to the big window overlooking the arena, and sure enough, as if she'd conjured them, the band was on stage, the sound of their guitar and drums growing louder.

The warm-up band played, and by the time they finished, the crowd was stamping their feet and calling for The Original Kings to come out.

Dash, as the lead singer, commanded the stage. Jordan had seen him evolve over the years, from a young boy performing in random bars to the man and star performer he was now. She put her problems away, letting herself sing, clap, and dance to the music, losing herself and her problems.

Linc was by her side, enjoying watching his brother with all the pride of an older sibling. His hands often came to Jordan's shoulders, his lips settling on her neck, causing shivers of awareness to ripple through her in the dark room, lit only by the lights of the band.

Her nipples grew tight and desire lit a flame inside her. God, she wished relationships were as simple as moments like they shared tonight.

When the lights came on, everyone was on a high from the performance, and they were talking loudly because their ears were ringing from the blaring sound of the music for the last couple of hours.

They made their way downstairs to the room where the band's meet and greet was to be held. People from all the boxes and those who'd won tickets courtesy of music stations and online sites waited for their time with members of the band.

Everyone talked over each other, and Jordan was uncomfortable with the crowds, needing air. "I'm going to find a chair and sit," she said in Linc's ear because it was the only way for him to hear her.

"Let's go into the outer room. It's quieter there." He grasped her hand and led the way.

She followed, working their way past the groups of people until they found the door and stepped into the outer connecting room. The sounds immediately dimmed, and she could hear herself think again.

She pressed her palms against her ears and patted them hard. "My God. This night has been insane!" She knew she was still talking too loudly and laughed.

"I like seeing you happy like this." Linc looked at her intently, his stare steady.

God, he was gorgeous. She loved that he hadn't shaved completely, the scruff of beard on his handsome face so appealing.

Suddenly she remembered what she had to tell him, and she sobered, feeling the grin on her face dimming. Before she could react, a male voice called her name. Thinking it was one of the Kingston brothers, she turned, shocked to see Collin Auerbach, her ex, walking up to her, a pregnant woman by his side.

Bile rose up in her throat, and Linc, who had met Collin years ago when she'd started dating him, slid a steadying arm behind her back.

But she wanted to handle this herself, without Collin knowing his presence brought back painful memories. Or that he affected her at all, and she pulled away to stand on her own. She knew that if she wasn't pregnant now, she wouldn't be thrown by his presence at all.

He strode up to her, looking every bit the preppy guy she'd known, with his light brown hair and caramel eyes, wearing slacks and a long-sleeve shirt. His outfit was too conservative for a concert. His wife, in her black pants and fitted maternity top, looked at her curiously. She clearly had no idea who Jordan was.

"Jordan! It's been a long time," Collin said.

It hadn't been long enough as far as she was concerned. She treated him to a forced smile. "Collin. I didn't think concerts were your thing."

"They're more Naomi's. She loves The Original Kings and I got us box seats. She's dying to meet Dash Kingston." His gaze came to Linc's.

The two men didn't run in the same circles, so they hadn't met up since the early days of Collin's relationship with Jordan. But from Collin's expression, he obviously recognized him.

"Aah, you two are still close, huh? And Dash Kingston is your brother. What do you say you get us to the front of the VIP line? You know, for an old friend?" He let out a laugh, as if he truly meant what he said.

"You have got to be kidding me. How about I escort you out?" Linc asked through clenched teeth.

Jordan put a calming hand on his arm. She did not want a scene.

"Collin? What's going on? Are you going to introduce me?" his wife asked.

"Yes, Collin. Why don't you introduce us?" Jordan asked with sugary sweetness in her tone.

"And while you're at it, why don't you give her the history of your relationship?" Linc said the one thing sure to send Collin running.

And it worked if his panicked expression was anything to go by.

"Honey, let's go. The line is long and I'm not feeling well." He glared at Linc, then turned to Jordan. "I thought enough time had passed that we could be civil."

"Never," she said through clenched teeth.

He grabbed his wife's hand and pulled her away, heading out of the room, Naomi complaining the entire time because he'd promised her she'd meet Dash Kingston.

Jordan let out a long breath and shook her head. "I swear to God, of all the nerve." It wasn't like Collin didn't know what had happened with her pregnancy, either.

About a month after she'd lost the baby, she'd sent him an email letting him know because she sensed it was the right thing to do, no matter how much of an asshole he'd been. She hadn't heard back. She'd been young and stupid and here she was again. Pregnant by a man who she knew had concerns about having children and whose life she worried she wouldn't fit into long-term.

"Hey, are you okay?" Linc asked.

She forced herself to meet his worried stare. "I'm fine and he's still an asshole."

"There you guys are!" Aurora walked over with Chloe beside her. "Hasn't tonight been incredible?"

Jordan smiled. "It has been." A wave of dizziness washed over her, and she barely held herself up with the heels of her shoes wobbling a bit.

She shot Chloe a nervous look, and she must have seen something in Jordan's expression that told her what to do. "Linc, come on. Want to introduce you to someone."

He grumbled but nodded. "Fine. I'll be right back."

As soon as he turned his back, she glanced at Aurora. "I need to sit down."

Looking concerned, Aurora looked around and pointed toward two chairs in the corner. "Come on."

Aurora waited as Jordan sat down, grateful to be off her feet. Her head spun and of course the nausea rose with it.

"Can I get you something? Maybe a drink? Club soda? Water?" Aurora asked.

"Maybe some club soda." The bubbles might help settle her stomach.

Aurora smiled. "I'll be right back."

Jordan leaned her head back against the wall and closed her eyes. A few minutes and maybe all these symptoms would go away.

"I'm back."

Jordan heard Aurora's voice, but she kept her eyes closed, not ready to deal with the dizziness.

"When I was pregnant, I lived on sour sucking candies to help the nausea. You should try those,"

Aurora said.

"You're pregnant?" Linc's voice had Jordan's eyelids opening fast. He stood behind his sister, his eyes huge in disbelief.

If Jordan's stomach was churning before, there were no words for what she was feeling now. "Linc—"

"Oh, God, I'm sorry!" Aurora's eyes filled with tears. "I didn't mean for him to overhear."

"It's okay. Honest." She sought to reassure the young woman. Meanwhile, Linc still stared at her, shock clearly not allowing him to process what he'd heard.

Aurora shook her head. "I'm going to... I guess I'll just go." She spun around and headed back into the VIP room.

With no choice but to face things head on, Jordan rose to her feet.

"You're pregnant," Linc said again, his voice hard.

At his harsh tone, she began to panic, breaking into a sweat, the dizziness worse. "I was going to tell you tonight."

"How?"

She blinked at the question. "Excuse me? I would think you could figure it out yourself. Maybe that ancient condom we used the first time?"

A muscle ticked in his jaw and all her fears rose to the surface. Another man who couldn't handle the reality of getting her pregnant. Hadn't she just seen Collin and his *pregnant* wife? Jordan was good enough to fuck but not good enough to stand by when things got tough.

And as Linc's silence went on, her mother's words came back to her:

You aren't family. I'm just reminding you of your place. One day that man you call your best friend is going to find a woman to marry, and where will that leave you?

"Shit," he muttered, running an agitated hand through his hair.

She stiffened. "Don't worry about it. This baby isn't your problem. *I'm* not your problem," she said, desensitizing herself the same way she had all those years ago with her ex. "Even if you wrote me a check like Collin or your father, I wouldn't take it." She barely recognized the robotic voice coming out of her mouth, but sounding numb was better than showing him her pain.

Her words seemed to jolt him out of his state of shock. "Jordan—"

She didn't stick around to hear what he had to say. She brushed past him and ran out the door.

Chapter Eleven

C HLOE DRAGGED LINC to meet a friend of hers who it turned out he already knew and disliked. A guy who tried to push an investment on him, here. At his brother's concert. Annoyed, Linc told the man to call him at the office to make an appointment and walked away, heading back to the spot where he'd left Jordan and Aurora. He'd be sure to tell Jordan not to put the man through when he called.

As Linc crossed the room, he realized the women weren't where he'd left them, but he caught sight of Jordan sitting in a chair, eyes closed, her head tipped back against the wall. He strode toward her just as Aurora stepped in front of Jordan, her back to Linc, a cup in her hand.

"When I was pregnant, I lived on sour sucking candies to help the nausea. You should try those," Aurora said to Jordan.

Jesus fuck. She was *pregnant?*

"You're pregnant?" Shock blanked out all common sense, and he blurted out the question.

Jordan's eyelids flew open, her gaze meeting his,

panic etched across her features. "Linc–"

"Oh, God, I'm sorry! I didn't mean for him to overhear," Aurora said, her voice shaking.

"It's okay. Honest," Jordan said in an attempt to soothe his obviously distraught sister.

But Linc didn't glance over. His attention remained on Jordan as he waited for her to deny it, to tell him he'd heard wrong or misunderstood.

"I'm going to… I guess I'll just go." Aurora spun around and headed back into the VIP room, leaving them alone.

Jordan rose unsteadily to her feet.

"You're pregnant," Linc said. Again, he heard the harshness in his tone, but all he could think about was the fact that kids were the last thing he'd ever wanted or planned.

She nodded. "I was going to tell you tonight."

"How?" If he had to name one thing he was careful about, it was using protection.

"Excuse me?" she asked, straightening her shoulders.

If looks could kill, he'd be dead on the spot.

"I would think you could figure that one out yourself. Maybe that ancient condom we used the first time?" she reminded him with no lack of sarcasm.

Son of a bitch, he thought, clenching his jaw. He'd been so hot, so eager to get inside her he hadn't cared what kind of protection he'd used as long as he was covered.

How the fuck did he process this? He'd been fifteen when he'd discovered his father was cheating. Seventeen when the man had slapped him on the shoulder and said, "Always wrap up, son. You don't want to end up with a kid you don't want," before Linc went out on a date one night. Not to mention finding out about Aurora about a month ago. But even before he learned his father had gotten his secretary pregnant and abandoned the baby, Linc had promised himself he wouldn't bring kids into the world. Never wanted them to end up miserable like he and his siblings had.

"Shit," he said louder than he should have, running a frustrated, angry hand through his hair.

"Don't worry about it. This baby isn't your problem. *I'm* not your problem." Jordan's voice brought him back to the present.

He'd never seen the blank look on her face before, and a sudden rush of fear ran through him. A different kind of fear than when he'd overheard she was pregnant with his baby. He simply couldn't get ahold of all his emotions. They were too big. Too panic-inducing.

"Even if you wrote me a check like Collin or your father, I wouldn't take it," she spat.

Oh, shit. Her words shook him to his core, and he

realized exactly what his reaction had done. "Jordan–"

She looked past him and rushed for the door. A large group of people was entering, but she managed to barrel through them, and though he attempted to go after her, the crowd of fans here to see the band was too big, too rowdy.

And when he finally stepped out of the room, he looked up and down the hallway, but he didn't see Jordan. There were so many people lined up against the wall he couldn't hope to find her. And with an exit sign at both ends, he had no idea which way she'd gone.

"Son of a bitch!" He slammed his palm against the wall, the pain excruciating, but he didn't care.

Pulling his phone from his pocket, he dialed Max, who waited in the town car in a nearby lot.

The man answered on the first ring. "Hi, Max. Have you heard from Jordan?"

"No, Mr. Kingston."

He clenched the cell tighter in his hand. "If she happens to call you, contact me immediately. I need to know she's safe."

"Of course. Is there anything else I can do?"

Linc groaned. "No. If she doesn't call you for a ride, I'm sure she'll take an Uber. Do me a favor? In five minutes, start driving around. I'll meet you at the same exit where you dropped us off. Thank you." He disconnected the call.

He intended to meet Jordan back at her apartment and discuss things more rationally, but he needed to let his family know he was leaving or else they'd worry.

He didn't explain his reasons for rushing out, but he did take the time to pull Aurora into a reassuring hug. "You didn't do anything wrong."

"But it was Jordan's place to tell you." She blinked back tears.

He had a feeling she was afraid she'd lose the family she'd just found. "I overheard you. You didn't intentionally tell me. Now please try and enjoy the rest of the night. I'm going to find her and we'll talk."

He glanced at Chloe, who obviously also knew about Jordan's pregnancy, and she stepped up to wrap an arm around Aurora's shoulder. "Come on. Dash and the guys are finishing up. Let's go hang out with them, okay?"

He nodded his thanks to Chloe, who smiled reassuringly as she led Aurora away.

"Linc? Is everything okay?" his mother asked.

He met her concerned gaze. "It will be. But I have a feeling I'm going to need to talk to you soon. It's too complicated to get into now."

She narrowed her eyes. "Well, now I am worried."

He patted her hand. "Don't be. I just need to fix some things I screwed up." He just hoped like hell

Jordan was open to listening.

He made his way down the escalators at the Garden, found the VIP exit he'd told Max to park near, then called his driver and met up with him.

"Did you hear from Ms. Greene?" Max asked.

"No." Linc had continuously checked his phone.

Once he was in the car and could concentrate without weaving his way through people, he called her, but it went straight to voicemail.

Next, he texted her: *I fucked up. I'm coming over to talk.*

He kept an eye on the screen, but it didn't show she'd seen it. Either she was ignoring him or she'd changed her settings not to show other people she'd read her messages.

Throughout the ride uptown, his stomach churned with concern. She'd run off by herself, upset. His shock had worn off, as had the thoughts he'd let fester in the back of his mind for years. He'd had a knee-jerk reaction to words he'd never thought to hear and responded like a complete jackass.

He wasn't proud of himself, and he was worried about what he'd done to Jordan's feelings, knowing he'd been no better than Collin the asshole. He curled his hands into fists and wished the time would pass faster, but eventually they pulled up in front of her building.

"Hang out, Max?"

"Sure thing, Mr. Kingston."

"Thank you." He opened the door and slid out, rushing inside.

The doorman greeted him on sight with a friendly nod, which meant Jordan hadn't put him on a not-allowed-to-come-up list. "Hi, Jerry. Can you please tell Ms. Greene I'm here?"

"I'm sorry, Mr. Kingston. She's out tonight. She left earlier and I haven't seen her since." The man sitting behind the desk in a black long-sleeve collared shirt shrugged in apology.

Linc narrowed his eyes. "Is there any chance you took a break and missed her?"

The middle-aged man shook his head. "Sorry. I've been here all night. Although I could use a break now," he said with a laugh Linc couldn't bring himself to return.

"Thanks." Linc slapped his hand on the desk and headed back to the car.

He climbed in. "Let me think for a few minutes, please."

Max nodded.

Where could Jordan have gone?

Her sister lived in Westchester County, where she had a job as a court clerk. Jordan might have taken a car there. He had Claire's number in his phone in case of an emergency, and he looked up her name, hitting send on the number.

A quick conversation and Linc struck out there, too. He had to tap-dance his way around not being able to reach Jordan on the phone but convincing Claire her sister was fine.

Friends? Jordan's social circle was small. She hadn't kept in touch with high school friends. Most of her college people had moved out of state, and though she was friendly with some of the office staff, he didn't think she'd confide in anyone there. Any other friends he didn't know well enough to call.

He drummed his fingers on the seat beside him. That left her mother, he thought, with a loud groan. There was a fifty-fifty shot Jordan would go to the one woman who would only say, *I told you so*, if Jordan told her the truth. And if she had gone to her mom, there was no way Tamara would let him in.

He'd fucked up so badly, he'd become the man he'd never wanted to be, reacting like his father. He hadn't thrown money at the situation, but he hadn't stepped up like a man. The man he wanted to be.

Running a hand over his face, then through his hair, he knew he had no choice but to go home, keep calling and texting. And hope she eventually responded.

★ ★ ★

JORDAN TOLD THE Uber she'd called to drive around but head toward the address she'd put into the app, her parents' house in Queens. She needed time to pull herself together before she faced her mother.

All the *I told you so's* were going to hurt, mostly because this was Linc they were talking about, and despite her fears, she'd so wanted to trust him. And his reaction had been like a punch in the gut. Or the heart. Basically both. She could have gone to her sister's house, but a big part of her wanted her mother.

When she'd been pregnant the first time, she'd been young and too afraid to admit the truth to her mom. She'd lost the baby before finding the courage to tell her, and she'd kept it hidden. But she was ready to stand up for herself and her choices now. No matter the consequences.

Finally the car pulled up to her parents' house, a small two-bedroom, two-bathroom house. She'd enjoyed growing up here, the warmth and the love. Despite her complaining about her mother's feelings about Linc, her mom loved her and only wanted to protect her from being hurt.

Maybe Jordan should have listened.

She thanked the driver, opened the door, and stepped out of the car, slamming the door shut. For safety's sake, she waited until she exited the car to turn off her phone, but she'd shut the sound and vibration, not wanting to talk to Linc. And she'd seen him start to text almost as soon as she finally left the venue.

Realizing she'd come here in a rock concert outfit and shoes with no change of clothes, she muttered a low curse, but she'd make do. She rushed up the path leading to the house and rang the bell. The curtain moved on the window beside the door. Thank goodness her parents liked to stay up late, she thought, as the door opened and her mother stood in the entryway.

Wearing a long caftan with a pretty pattern, her blonde hair pulled back in a bun, her mother glanced at her, her unlined face worried. Despite how hard she'd worked, Tamara had beautiful skin, and she had pride in her appearance. Once her father's electrical business took off, she'd been able to quit her housekeeping job, and she turned her knitting hobby into a business, selling items on Etsy.

"Jordan, what's wrong?" her mom asked.

With the burden of secrets on her shoulders, she met her mother's gaze. "I'm pregnant with Linc's baby," she said as tears filled her eyes.

Which was okay. She was finally safe to let them fall because Linc wasn't around to judge her. And her mother pulled Jordan into her arms.

A little while later, her mom had shooed Jordan's father to the bedroom, made them both a cup of tea, and they sat facing each other across the table.

"Please don't say I told you so." Jordan poured some milk and added sugar, wrapping her hands around the warm mug.

Her mother let out a heartfelt sigh. "It's too late to do any good anyway."

Jordan nodded in agreement. She decided it was time to admit it all. "Mom, this isn't the first time I've gotten pregnant."

"What?"

Looking down at the light-colored tea, Jordan drew a deep breath and told her mother about what had happened with Collin. "And it was my fault. I had a migraine and skipped the pill, but this time, with Linc, we used protection." It was old but there was no point in telling her mother that. "I guess I'm just one of those fertile people." She let out a wry laugh.

Her mother reached out, and Jordan put her hand in her mom's calloused one. "Why didn't you tell me?"

Jordan swallowed hard. "I knew you thought I was dating above my means and you were so insistent, both with Linc and Collin, I couldn't face your disappointment." Tears pooled in her eyes again, and she used a napkin to dab at the moisture, not wanting her heavy makeup all over her face.

"Oh, honey." Her mother's expression crumbled, her pain for her daughter obvious and so needed. "I feel terrible. I was looking out for you. I thought I could protect you, but I never meant to make it so you couldn't come to me when you needed me most." She curled her fingers tighter around Jordan's hand.

"I get it now, Mom. I know why you tried so hard to protect me." Jordan went on to explain how Collin had tried to pay her to get rid of the baby, and her mom cursed loudly.

"Now tell me what happened when you told Linc," her mother said.

"First you need to know about his father." Jordan revealed how Kenneth Kingston had gotten his secretary pregnant and paid her monthly for years instead of being a parent.

Her mom shook her head. "That man was always a selfish son of a bitch. Mrs. Kingston put up with too much from him if you ask me. Now what about Linc?"

Jordan pulled in a breath. "He overheard Aurora, his new sister, say something to me about being pregnant. I get he was in shock. But he repeated it twice and he sounded so angry." She'd wanted to curl into herself, but she refused to let him see how badly he was hurting her.

And then he'd asked *how*, which was the ultimate in stupid questions. But Collin had asked her the same thing, and that time she'd been at fault. All the memories had come crashing back, especially because she'd just run into him and his pregnant wife.

"So we stood there in silence except for the other voices in the room. And his face might as well have been carved in stone. And in my head, I heard your voice, telling me I wasn't part of their family, and I needed to know my place. And that one day he'd marry someone else."

She wiped at her eyes again, her mascara all over the napkin. "Then Linc cursed. And I lost it. I told him not to worry, that the baby wasn't his problem. That I wasn't his problem."

Her mother patted her hand. "That's my brave girl, standing up for herself. But—"

Jordan pushed the mug aside. "Wait. There's more. I topped it off and told him if he wrote me a check like Collin or his father, I wouldn't take it. Then I walked out … and here I am."

A few silent seconds ticked by as her mother clearly gathered her thoughts. "Has he tried to reach you?"

She nodded. "When I first left. Then I silenced my phone. And now it's turned off."

"Okay, good. Because you need time to think. How about I give you some clothes to change into, you wash up and get a good night's sleep? We can talk again in the morning. Sound good?"

"Yeah. It does." Jordan didn't think she'd get

much shut-eye, but she needed to be alone and process everything that had happened tonight.

Her mom rose from her seat and Jordan did the same. Walking around, her mother wrapped her arms around Jordan and pulled her close. Her scent was familiar and comforting, and she knew she'd done the right thing by coming home.

LINC DIDN'T SLEEP. Not well, at least. The only good news he'd had since Jordan walked out on him was a one-line text letting him know she was fine. That was all she'd said. *I'm fine.* She'd ignored everything he'd texted after, asking where she was and if they could talk, and his calls still went to voicemail. But he took comfort in the knowledge she'd thought to let him know she was safe. That meant no matter how big an ass he'd been, deep down she knew he'd worry about her.

Although he had no intention of letting a day pass without seeing her, whether she was at her parents' house or not, he had one stop to make first.

He felt like driving himself and headed to his mother's house for a serious conversation. After opening the gate and parking, he rang the bell, and since she'd been expecting him, his mother answered. They'd been out late last night, and she wasn't dressed up nor did she have on a full face of makeup, but she was still beautiful.

They settled in the large kitchen, which had recently been remodeled, with stainless steel appliances, white granite counters, and state-of-the-art ... everything.

She offered him something to eat but he declined. He'd eaten at home.

They sat on barstools at the center island, and he leaned an elbow on the granite. He wasn't sure how to approach the subject. Until he and Jordan talked, he had no intention of telling his mother she was pregnant. He hoped his sisters had kept the news to themselves.

"So you told me last night we needed to talk. What is it?" his mother asked.

"How do you feel about Jordan?" he asked, diving right in.

She tipped her head, confusion in her expression. "I'm not sure what you mean."

He let out a groan. "Okay, there's no easy way to ask this. Chloe mentioned to me that Jordan *isn't one of us*. That people in our so-called social circle consider her the maid's daughter and ... they look down on her."

He wasn't asking his mother these questions because he needed her approval before making things right with Jordan. Rather, he was asking because he wanted to counter any argument Jordan herself might have about them being together and having a future.

He knew he was getting ahead of himself. First he needed her to forgive him for his reaction to their big news. But Linc was a man who prepared for all situations before taking a leap. Another reason her pregnancy had been such a shock. He'd never considered the possibility.

He glanced at his mother, who looked like a woman trying to formulate her answer, and his stomach churned. Not for himself but because he wanted to be able to tell Jordan she'd be welcome in his family.

His mother clasped her hands together on the counter and blew out a long breath. "Are you asking how I feel or how other people feel?"

Was she hesitating to answer or was she really confused? Linc wasn't certain.

"I don't give a shit how the outside world thinks. I do, however, care about Jordan being treated with respect by everyone. And frankly I think this conversation is ridiculous in today's world, but I believe Chloe when she tells me that's how some people feel."

His mother nodded. "Unfortunately, there are people who come from money and think they're better than others. Your father being one of those people."

"Yes. He hated Jordan being a big part of my life."

And the fact that his father had been rude to her had put up yet another barrier between them.

His mother glanced down at her perfectly manicured nails before meeting his gaze. "But if you're asking how I feel, I've always liked Jordan. I think she's a lovely young woman who has been a good friend to you."

"She's more than a friend." He kept his eyes on his mother, wanting to gauge her reaction.

She blinked. "Oh. Oh! Well, that's a surprise. I guess I should have been paying more attention, because I had no idea!" Sudden awareness lit her expression. "And *that's* why you want to know how I feel about her."

He inclined his head, nodding.

An unexpected smile lifted his mother's lips. "Sounds like I should be asking you the same question. Except I don't think you'd be here if it was just a casual thing."

At her calm acceptance, the tension in his shoulders eased. "It's far from casual. And you need to know I'm not asking you for myself, because I'm all in no matter how anyone else feels. But I would like to be able to tell Jordan she's a welcome part of our family."

He'd never sensed any issues coming from his mother, and he already knew his siblings liked Jordan.

But as Chloe had said, he was a man. And guys didn't always think like women when it came to this shit. Social status, money, who you were born to. None of it made a damned bit of difference to him. Hadn't Beck been his close friend in college before a woman came between them?

And Jordan had always been his best friend. He should have realized sooner that she was his everything.

"Linc, I always liked Jordan and she has always fit in here. She's always been welcome. As for the snobs who we are forced to deal with outside of our home? If they don't accept her, then I have no use for them."

Reaching out, she covered his hand with hers. "So how serious are you two?"

It was all he could do not to tell her everything, but he needed to wait. "It's very serious."

"Enough for me to give you your grandmother's diamond? I know how much you loved her, and the stone is a Kingston family heirloom. I can't think of a better way to show her she's welcome."

And this was why he loved his mother. Standing, he took two steps and pulled her into a hug.

Chapter Twelve

L INC INPUT JORDAN'S parents' address into his GPS and drove there, his heart pounding hard in his chest. He didn't know if he had the right words to fix things between them. He only knew he had to find them or he would never be happy again and he'd lose the person who meant the most to him. Not to mention, he'd have to live with knowing he'd hurt her. And she was pregnant with his baby. So he had to undo the damage he'd done.

His cell rang, and with the buttons on his steering wheel, he took the call without checking who was on the other end. "Hello?"

"Linc? It's Wallace." The connection wasn't solid, and static sounded in the background.

"Jesus, Wallace. What the fuck? How could you up and disappear?" He gripped the wheel and did his best to pay attention to the road and the signs.

"I'm sorry. I didn't know Kenneth would go to such extremes, and when I found out, I didn't know what else to do." The man's voice trembled.

Linc shook his head. "Talk to me and start at the

beginning."

The other man let out a long, wailing sound and Linc cringed. "Your father was my best friend. I would have done anything for him, and when he got his diagnosis, he was devastated," Wallace said.

"I wouldn't know. He didn't confide in me." If anything, Kenneth had kept Linc at arm's length, and since Linc never wanted to be close to him, he hadn't cared.

The dementia had been a blow, but Linc never wanted his father to get sick or die.

"Your father knew how you felt about him. Hell, he even understood. You all put Melly first. He got that. But the business was Kenneth's baby." Wallace paused. "And as much as he wanted his oldest son, the only son who cared about Kingston Enterprises as much as he did, in the business? He was envious of your success and worried he'd be seen as weak once he began showing more signs of his illness."

Linc put his signal on and took the next exit. "So what did you do?"

"Some creative accounting and I moved money around. I opened a separate account for Kenneth to use to make deals. It allowed him to feel in control and like the king of real estate he used to be. It let him avoid lenders and people who'd notice his diminishing abilities."

Linc shook his head, surprised Wallace's underlying rationale had been friendship, not greed. But Linc knew how much his father owed Beck, and even Kenneth had realized he'd needed collateral. So where was Wallace in all this?

"You have to believe me," the other man said. "I never thought Kenneth would make a deal without my knowledge. Or be crazy enough to offer Beckett Daniels a piece of the company if he couldn't come up with the money."

Linc groaned. "So what's your plan? To hide out in the Maldives for the rest of your life?"

"Unless you don't plan on pressing charges. I don't know what I'd be liable for but…" Wallace's voice trailed off, giving Linc time to think.

Friendship. Wallace had done it all for friendship and to help Linc's father retain his dignity. Under these circumstances, how could Linc hold him criminally responsible?

"I'm not pressing charges," he said. "You took care of my father, albeit in an extremely stupid way." But Linc couldn't keep him on. Not when he couldn't trust the man's judgment or decision-making. "Just resign and we'll call it even."

"Thank you." Relief suffused Wallace's voice. "I can't imagine not being able to easily see my boys."

Linc knew his wife had passed away a couple of

years ago, but he had adult children here in the States. "Wallace, just come home. I've got to go."

"Goodbye, Lincoln. Thank you."

Shaking his head, he disconnected the call. How his father had inspired such loyalty was beyond Linc's understanding.

But business and his father were the last things Linc needed to be concentrating on. His focus should be on much more important matters. Like convincing Jordan of his feelings and sincerity.

As he drove, he considered everything he needed to say. Thirty minutes later, he pulled up in front of her parents' modest home. He hadn't been here before. Not because Jordan had been embarrassed, but they'd both decided it was better not to upset her mother by pushing their friendship in her face when she so clearly disapproved.

He climbed out and made his way up the walk and faced the doorbell with dread. Dealing with Tamara Greene wouldn't be easy.

Before he lifted his hand to ring, he saw movement of the drapes on the side window, and then the door opened and Jordan's mother stood in the entry. Obviously she'd seen him first.

Tamara wore a pair of jeans and a peach-colored blouse. With her blonde hair and blue eyes, she reminded him of a slightly harder version of her daughter.

Growing up, he'd always liked her. She'd been good to him, making sure he and his siblings had cookies and milk after school and even helping with homework if his mother wasn't around. In fact, she hadn't become gruff and abrupt with him until high school.

"Hello, Mrs. Greene."

"Lincoln, it's about time you showed up." Instead of letting him inside, she stepped out to join him. "Now you listen to me, young man."

He blinked, and since he wasn't stupid, he did as she said and waited for her to speak.

"I always liked you. You were a good boy, respectful, and smart. It wasn't until I realized my daughter had a crush on you that I knew I had to do something about your friendship. I couldn't let her get hurt by … well, to be frank, people like your father and the country club crowd."

Jordan had had a crush on him in high school? That was news to him, but he couldn't deny the jolt of pleasure that hit him as he found out.

"I understand your feelings about my father," he said. "But nobody else in my family has ever or will ever hurt Jordan."

Tamara narrowed her gaze. "Except you."

He winced because the truth stung. "I'm here to

fix things."

She settled her hands on her hips. "It had better be the right way, because no grandbaby of mine is going to be born without his parents being married. Not when they love each other like you and Jordan do."

Shocked by her words, he cocked his head to the side. "How do you know how we feel?" Oh, Linc knew he loved Jordan. He'd had the entire ride here to put his feelings into words as he figured out what he would say to her, and love was at the center of his argument.

"Best friends, my ass," Tamara muttered.

He bit back a laugh. He'd always liked her bluntness.

"Nobody spends the amount of time together you two do without having real feelings," she went on. "Now I admit I'm still worried, but given the situation, I've decided to trust you. Now good luck getting my daughter to do the same."

She stepped aside and gestured for him to come in, and he followed her into the small entryway.

"I'm going to convince her to hear you out. I suggest you figure out what you're going to say," Tamara said.

Linc stared at her retreating back, marveling at the woman's honesty. She didn't hold back and he respected that.

He made his way into the family room to his left and walked around, looking at the family photos on the mantel and the shelves while he waited for Jordan.

JORDAN SAT ON the bed in the room she'd shared with her sister, wearing an old tee shirt of her dad's and a pair of her mother's sweatpants. Her hair was wild from the spray she'd used to hold the waves she'd made last night for the concert. And despite having washed her face and used a ton of makeup remover, when she'd brushed her teeth, she'd noticed she still had black streaks beneath her eyes. Lovely.

But it wasn't like she was going anywhere. She'd decided to stay here for a couple of days. Let Linc deal with a temp as his assistant and see how he liked being without her.

She lifted her knees and wrapped her arms around them, needing the pressure against her stomach because, of course, she was nauseous again. The male got a female pregnant, but it was the woman who had to suffer with all the side effects. So unfair.

Not to mention, she'd skipped breakfast and hoped she felt better soon, because despite how crappy she was feeling, she was also weirdly hungry.

A knock sounded on her door. "Come in."

Her mother walked into the room and stood by

her bed. "How are you feeling? Any better?" she asked, concern in her tone.

Jordan shook her head. "Not yet. I did get a few crackers down though."

"Good." Her mother smiled. "You have company."

Jordan's stomach did a complete flip, and she was lucky she didn't throw up. "What? Who?"

"Don't play dumb. Now get up and wash your face before you go downstairs. You can't help being pale, but there's no reason to look like a raccoon when you face Linc."

Jordan narrowed her gaze. "What is with this sudden pushing me toward him? All you ever wanted was to keep us apart."

Her mother shook her head. "Wrong. I wanted to protect you." She lowered herself onto the bed beside Jordan's bent legs. "Now tell me something and don't even think of lying to your mother. Do you love him?"

Shocked by the question, Jordan looked everywhere but at her mom. "Will you judge me if I say I do?" Because she'd probably loved him for years.

Though, after the way he'd reacted to her being pregnant, it killed her to admit the truth. Considering Linc knew what she'd been through with Collin when she'd been pregnant, last night he'd still thrown that same shocked, horrified attitude in her face. Her stomach spun at the painful memory.

Her mother sighed. "There's no accounting for love, so no, I won't judge you. As hard as I tried to prevent your pain, here we are." Her mother ran a soothing hand over Jordan's arm. "I listened to you last night. I heard you. And I thought about how things played out between you and Linc."

"Just what are you saying?"

"That when he heard you were pregnant, you shocked him. You didn't have a chance to lay the groundwork and soften the blow. Imagine hearing the news in a room full of people and not expecting it."

She hugged her legs tighter. "I know because I found out almost the same way." Aurora had suggested it, and next thing Jordan knew, she was in a public bathroom stall, three pregnancy tests on the floor in front of her.

And she'd completely freaked out.

"I see you understand my point," her mom said. "And despite how hard I've been on you two all these years, you've stood by his side. I have to believe it's because you saw something special in him."

"I did," Jordan whispered.

"Well, I realize I was basing my feelings on his father's attitude and behavior." Her mother drew a deep breath. "And your father and I talked late into the night, and he helped me to see reason."

Jordan blinked in surprise. "Dad knows I'm pregnant?" she asked in shock.

Her mother shot her a look. "Of course. We don't keep secrets. He'd have talked to you this morning, but you were sleeping when he left on an emergency work call."

With her head spinning and Linc downstairs, Jordan didn't know whether to run to him for emotional support or hide under the covers until he went away. She knew what her heart wanted, and God, that scared her.

"Ask yourself why he's here and don't tell me you think he wants to pay you off." Apparently her mother wasn't finished with her newfound wisdom.

Jordan flinched because she never should have said those words to him. He'd been in shock, as her mother had said.

And she'd let the past dictate her reaction. "I can't believe you, of all people, are trying to convince me to find the good in Linc," Jordan muttered.

"I always saw the good in him. My concerns were never about him." Her mother patted her knee. "Now go clean up and I'll tell him you'll be right down."

"What about your concerns about me not fitting into his world?" Jordan asked, sliding out of bed.

Her mom let out a sigh as if the answer were obvious. But it wasn't. Not to Jordan.

"Where have you been all these years?" her mom asked. "You've been by his side," she said before Jordan could answer. "I simply didn't see the truth staring me in the face. Linc Kingston has your back. Now ask yourself if you can forgive him for being a jerk, because take it from someone who knows. It won't be the last time you'll have to forgive him for stupid behavior."

Her mother's grin lightened the mood, and Jordan couldn't help but smile back. "Only if he grovels nicely."

Her mom laughed, then stood up and walked out the door.

Jordan glanced in the mirror above the dresser and groaned. She could wash the black eye makeup away, but there wasn't much more she could do to fix her pale face. Linc would have to take her or leave her.

FROM THE ENTRY to the family room, Jordan watched Linc pace the carpeted floor. He wore a pair of dark jeans and a cream-colored Henley top, looking as sexy as ever. It wasn't fair. She'd done her best to pull herself together, but she was still pale, her eyes red and puffy from crying, and her hair pulled into a messy bun on top of her head.

Here goes nothing, she thought. "Linc?"

He turned toward her, his face filled with relief at the sight of her. He took her in, consuming her, those eyes traveling from head to toe, and she couldn't help but be self-conscious. With no desire to put last night's tight outfit back on, she still wore her borrowed sweats and tee.

"I know, not my best look." She gestured to her mismatched outfit. "But I came straight here last night, and I had to borrow something to wear."

He shoved his hands into his pants pockets. "Actually I think you look cute."

She did her best not to cringe at the description and folded her arms across her chest.

"Can we sit?" he asked.

She walked to the sofa and settled into the corner, well aware her body language and attitude gave off a keep-your-distance vibe.

Proving he knew her well, he sat one cushion away from her, providing her with the distance she needed as she waited in silence for him to speak.

He cleared his throat and looked into her eyes. "I didn't handle things well last night and I'm sorry."

He owned his actions, and she not only appreciated it, she knew what it said about his character. None of which meant she would let him off easily. A big part of her needed to express her feelings so he really understood what he'd done.

"Complete understatement," she said with a hint of defiance in her tone. "Should we start with you asking me how *it* happened? Your angry tone of voice?" She snapped her fingers. "Oh, I know. How about when you said, *shit*? As if the worst thing in the world had happened to you?"

Ducking his head, he admitted, "None of them were my finest moment."

Although she gave him credit. He didn't use him being caught off guard as an excuse. But she was well aware that how he'd found out she was pregnant factored into his negative reaction, something her mother had forced her to face.

Jordan blew out a long breath and sighed. "Look, I know you were in shock. You overheard Aurora and it was the last thing you expected to hear."

"That doesn't make it right," he muttered.

She nodded in agreement. "No, it doesn't. But I shouldn't have lumped you in with your father and Collin, either."

His wince told her how hard the comparison had hit him, and she couldn't help but feel bad.

"I know I wasn't fair. You'd never throw a check at a problem like this." She'd hurled the accusation as a means of self-protection, before he could treat her the way Collin had.

The amazing thing was, Linc's silence and lack of

emotion had sliced through her worse than her ex's financial solution.

Linc's body stiffened. "Jordan, you are not a problem and neither is our *baby*." As he said the word, his entire expression softened. "We're having a baby," he repeated in awe, almost as if he'd just now realized what her being pregnant meant, and he was now happy about it.

"I don't understand." She shook her head, confused. "We both know you were against having kids." Her stomach churned at the reminder. "You said you didn't want them to relive your childhood in any way."

"And they won't," he said, his tone full of certainty. "No baby of ours will relive the kind of upbringing I had. Not with us as parents."

She blinked back tears and trembled at the swell of emotion rushing through her. Reaching out, he rubbed his thumb over her bottom lip, and it was all she could do not to wrap her body around him and put last night behind her.

Could she?

Should she trust his change of heart?

"I want you to listen carefully and hear everything I'm about to say. Now, are you paying attention?" His firm tone had her sitting up straighter and focusing.

He slid closer, picking up her hand and holding it in his. "When I said I didn't want children, I imagined marrying and having them with someone like Angelica, who I couldn't see ever getting along with long-term. Those were the kind of women who came and went, but I didn't let any of them in, and none stayed for long."

"I know," she whispered.

"But I finally understand why. I was so insistent on not wanting to lose what *we* shared that I was blind to what we actually *were*. To what we *are*." His blue eyes were dark, his voice laced with sincerity, his gaze warm and full of what she thought was hope.

"And what is that?" she asked, her voice thick. Her heart rate picked up speed, and she felt the rapid beat in her chest.

His dizzying smile nearly brought her to her knees.

"We're best friends." He cupped her face in his hands and held her gaze with his. "Soul mates." He brushed his lips gently over hers. "And very much in love," he said, sealing their mouths together.

She kissed him, falling into their desire. He smelled so good, and now she did push herself up and settle in his lap, facing him and wrapping herself around him like she'd been dying to do earlier. His erection settled against her sex, and she moaned, their tongues sliding against each other, the kiss going on for a long while, until she broke their connection.

They still had more to discuss. "You're saying you

love me."

"Yes, Jordan. I love you," he said in a deep, honest voice.

She bit down on her damp bottom lip, then asked, "And what if I wasn't pregnant?"

He grinned. "Then I'd knock you up as soon as possible. Now isn't there something you want to tell me?"

Although she loved his answer, they had one more thing to talk about. "Not yet." She cleared her throat. "We both know I have issues with how I fit into your world. Things my mother said, that Angelica said, and how people at that club look at me." She shook her head. "I've always been able to handle it because I was an outsider, but I don't want to put you in the middle. Not to mention, what will your mother say? She's always been nice to me as your friend, but as your girlfriend?"

His unexpected laughter had her stiffening.

"Relax," he said. "I'm not laughing at you. I had a long talk with my mother already, and she had the perfect way to help me convince you that you are one of us. And to hell with what anyone else says or thinks."

He shifted her up and slid his hand into his front jeans pocket, fishing around and returning with something in his closed hand.

"Do you remember my grandmother Cecile?" he asked.

She nodded. "Your father's mother. Of course. She was your favorite grandparent." Jordan recalled the times he'd spend with his grandma and tell her all about their talks whenever she saw him next.

"Well, she gave my father a diamond to set into an engagement ring for my mother. And unlike their marriage being awful, my grandparents loved each other very much. I forgot about them in light of my father's behavior and my mother's misery. But from now on, I choose to focus on the good this ring caused, and my mother offered it to me to give to you."

He opened his hand and revealed a large diamond ring Jordan used to see on his mother's finger, and she let out a gasp. "Linc!"

"We will have this reset especially for you, but first…" He lifted her by her waist and slid her to the sofa.

Taking her by surprise, he lowered himself to one knee. "Jordan Marie Greene, will you marry me?"

He'd apologized and proved himself in all the ways that mattered to her. And there was nothing she wanted more than to spend the rest of her life with this man who was, as he'd said, her best friend and soul mate.

"Yes. Yes!" she squealed, laughing.

"Sorry but I'm not putting this setting on your finger. We're starting out with good juju. As soon as we can, we'll have it reset." He rose to his feet and slid the ring back into his pocket.

Jordan had no problem with his plan.

"By the way, I would have asked for your parents' permission, but your mother already told me no grandchild of hers would be born without us being married. And while you were getting ready, she told me your father would approve."

Jordan groaned. "If you hadn't already come here with the ring in your pocket, I'd kill her."

"I heard that!" her mother called out from way too close by.

Both Jordan and Linc laughed.

"She really did a one-eighty about me," he said, speaking low.

Jordan sighed. "She wasn't able to keep us apart all these years. When she heard I was pregnant, her blinders came off."

"Well, I'm glad. I'd rather have her on our side. Now can we go? I'd really like to consummate this engagement," he whispered.

Popping up from the couch, she stood and grasped his hand. "Take me home. Now."

"Anything you want," he said and she knew he

meant it.

IN THE LAST two weeks, Jordan's life had changed. She accepted her place in Linc's life and let go of old insecurities, while he embraced their relationship publicly and enthusiastically, including the fact that he would become a father. Though Jordan worried about miscarrying, a trip to the obstetrician assured her she was healthy and there was no reason to anticipate a problem.

Now she sat in Linc's SUV with a scarf wrapped around her eyes as they headed … somewhere he didn't want her to see.

"Come on, give me a hint?" she asked after who knows how long listening to the radio, him humming, refusing to talk, and keeping her in suspense.

"Nope." But the car came to a stop and he shut the engine. "But you can take off the blindfold now."

She eagerly pulled off the silk scarf and blinked as she adjusted to the sunlight. When she gazed out her side window, a brand-new house set back on a massive plot of land came into view. It was a gorgeous brick Georgian-style manor home that rivaled the Kingston Estate in size and surrounding property.

"Where are we?" she asked, her mouth going dry.

"Ready to go in and take a look?" he asked, restarting the engine.

"That's not an answer," she informed him.

"It's a house."

She shook her head. "It's more like a mansion or an estate that five families could live in," she said, panicking as she realized what was happening.

He shrugged, taking it all in stride. The massive house, the acres of land. This was all normal to him.

"We're having a baby. We need the room." He put the car in drive and headed down a tree-lined road before turning onto a long driveway leading to the house.

Overwhelmed, Jordan curled a knee under her and twisted toward him. "Linc! You're going crazy. In the last two weeks, you moved me into your place, got me out of my lease, pulled off a huge dinner for both of our families, and bought and demanded my ring be sized and ready in twenty-four hours! Now we're looking at this massive house for sale? No. Just no!" she said, her voice rising.

He placed a calming hand on her knee. "Okay, I thought you might hyperventilate when you got a look at this place." He reached into the side of his seat and pulled out papers. "What about any of these?" he asked in a soothing voice. "They're more reasonable. We can work up to the estate."

Rolling her eyes, she accepted the Realtor pages

and used them to slap him on the arm before looking through the contents and relaxing at the more realistic places for them to live.

"I agree we need more space," she said. "But no more giving heart attacks, okay?" It was one thing to adjust to becoming a Kingston, another to buy this land and house.

Thank goodness he'd anticipated her reaction and had given her options. In the end, another two weeks after they started looking, they agreed on what Jordan still thought was a massive home not far from his family estate. The location satisfied his mother's need to be near her soon-to-be grandbaby and was only a half-hour drive for Jordan's parents.

Since Linc wanted to do some renovations on the house, Jordan convinced him to let them stay in the city until she was seven months pregnant, giving her time to adjust to their new normal without making so many changes at once.

As for getting married, neither one of them wanted to upstage Chloe, so they decided to wait until after his sister's wedding next month. Jordan wanted a small, intimate ceremony, and Linc seemed happy to keep the event to their families only.

Tonight, he was at the gym in the building, doing his workout, and Jordan had decided to cook dinner. She'd gotten used to his kitchen, and he'd accepted that she didn't want a housekeeper handling every meal. Although she had to admit, after long workdays, it was nice to come home to a fully prepared dinner that wasn't takeout or delivery.

Jordan wasn't the world's best cook but she could handle some basics, and she'd made them lasagna and garlic bread. Leaving it to cool a little, she went to change into a silky lounge set before Linc came back home.

LINC FINISHED HIS workout and made his way to the penthouse. He needed a hot shower, and then he looked forward to sitting down for dinner with his soon-to-be wife. Since the day in her mother's house when he'd apologized and bared his soul, he'd done everything he could to make Jordan happy and prove to her they had what it took to last forever.

At times, she thought he was moving too fast. More often he didn't think they were going fast enough. He wanted everything with her and he wanted it now. But he was learning the fine art of compromise. If it were up to him, he'd buy her the world. She didn't seem to want anything more than his love and a lifetime together, and that was only one of the things that made her so special.

He opened the door and let himself inside, kicking

off his sneakers near the door. The delicious aroma of garlic wafted through the apartment, and he went in search of Jordan. She wasn't in the kitchen, though dinner sat cooling on the counter.

He strode through the apartment and into the bedroom in time to see Jordan standing in a bra and panties, a light blue silk outfit laid out on the bed.

He took in her sexy profile, her long hair hanging over her shoulders and the barely visible swell of her belly holding his baby.

A desire so strong he couldn't contain it rushed through him. "Jordan."

She jumped at the sound of his voice and turned toward him. "I didn't hear you come in." Her gaze swept over him, and her eyes darkened with a need he recognized.

"You like me sweaty," he said in a gruff voice.

A teasing smile lifted her lips. "I like you any way I can get you. But I'm sure you're hungry, so if you want to jump in the shower, I'll get dinner on the table. I have to get dressed," she said, reaching for her shirt.

"Don't." He was starving, but not for food. He knew Jordan had spent time cooking, and he had every intention of eating whatever she'd prepared, but first he wanted to devour *her*.

He stalked toward her, catching her expression the minute she realized his intent. Her baby blues opened wide, and with a tempting smile, she unhooked her bra from behind. It slid down her arms, revealing her gorgeous breasts, which were slightly larger and a lot more tender than they'd been before.

He stopped in front of her, waiting as she hooked her fingers into the band of her panties and pulled them down her legs and kicked them aside.

She stood before him naked, beautiful, and all his.

He pulled his shirt, lifting it from the back collar and sliding it over his head and arms, tossing it across the room. He took care of his shorts, boxers briefs, then socks next.

Before she could react, he grabbed her around the waist, and together they toppled onto the bed. He came over her, making certain not to crush her in any way.

With his eyes on hers, he raised himself up, his cock settled at her entrance. She was wet for him, as she always was. "I love you, soon-to-be Mrs. Kingston."

Her smile lit up his life. "And I love you, Mr. Kingston."

As soon as he heard the words, he eased himself inside her, groaning at the perfection of her slick heat as he took her completely.

Afterwards, they lay in each other's arms, his hand settled on her belly. He was grateful for everything they'd found and finally recognized in each other.

"I don't want to move, ever," she said, curling deeper into his side.

"You don't ever have to."

Epilogue

One Month Later

OVER ONE HUNDRED and fifty guests filled the main room of the country club. White flowers lined either side of the aisle, and up front a beautiful white and gold arch stood where the couple would be married.

Jordan sat in the front row, waiting for the double doors to open and for Chloe's wedding to begin. Linc and his brothers were gathered in the entry room, looking handsome in their tuxedos. The bridesmaids and Chloe's maid of honor were waiting as well. Though Chloe had wanted to add Jordan to her entourage, Jordan declined, wanting Chloe to have her closest friends standing up for her. Besides, since Linc was walking his sister down the aisle, Jordan truly didn't mind being with the rest of the guests.

Word had spread about Jordan and Linc's engagement, in no small part because his mother had insisted a formal announcement be mailed out. Jordan knew it had been Melly's way of openly welcoming her, and she was grateful.

Glancing at her phone, she realized it was past the time when the wedding should have started. She smoothed her hand over the designer dress she'd had to have let out at the waist, because one morning she'd woken up and discovered she no longer had indentations on either side of her stomach. Excitement rippled through her as she settled her hand on her barely there belly.

Suddenly the doors she'd been watching began to open, and everyone rose to their feet, only for the wooden doors to slam shut again.

People began to whisper, then talk, asking each other what was happening. Jordan wondered herself and sent Linc a text.

Jordan: *What's wrong?*

A few minutes passed and his answer came.

Linc: *Can't find the groom. If he shows, I'm going to kill him before my sister can ruin her life with that son of a bitch.*

Jordan rose to her feet. Ignoring the people calling questions after her, she rushed up the aisle and out the doors to find Linc and his siblings. Chloe had her mother and friends to calm her.

Someone needed to talk the Kingston brothers down.

Thanks for reading! Chloe Kingston and Beck Daniels are up next in JUST ONE SCANDAL!

JUST ONE SCANDAL EXCERPT

*J*ILTED ON THE *day of my wedding. Of all the pathetic, clichéd things to happen*, Chloe Kingston thought with frustration and disgust. "How did I not see this coming?"

She fluffed her white ball gown dress, adjusting the tulle beneath the skirt, and sat down on the chair in the bridal suite of the hotel where her wedding was to be held.

She pulled a bottle of champagne out of the ice bucket and chugged down a healthy gulp of Dom Perignon straight from the bottle. Letting the bubbles settle, she repeated the action a couple of more times because she needed to get drunk. And on that thought, she took another hefty sip.

She was alone because she'd insisted she needed a few minutes by herself since getting *that* text. Her bridal party, consisting of her best friends, her sister, Aurora, and her brothers, because Owen had included them as his groomsmen, waited in the outer room. Impatiently if their loud voices were anything to go by. It had been hard to convince her mom to step out, along with her oldest brother, Linc, who Chloe had asked to walk her down the aisle.

Her father had passed away three months ago, and they hadn't been close. But she was glad he wasn't here to see this day. He'd be furious. Not because his daughter had been left at the altar but because he would have been embarrassed in front of friends, family, and business associates, and she couldn't deal with his reaction on top of everything else today. As it was, Chloe couldn't look at her mother's worried expression. Couldn't handle the pity in her friends' eyes or the fury in her brothers.

If there was one good thing about Owen ditching her via text message, it was that her brothers couldn't pound the man into the ground. And given the chance, they would. The Kingston siblings were nothing if not protective.

She glanced around the beautiful suite with plush chairs, makeup strewn around, her veil sitting on the counter, and wondered how she'd come to this point. She'd chosen who she thought was the perfect man. A tax attorney who never took risks, enjoyed staying home, and who'd promised to be faithful. He'd ticked off all the most important qualifications in her life, making her feel secure and comfortable and, most importantly, safe from being cheated on like her mother had been.

The screen on her phone sitting beside the headpiece said otherwise: *I'm sorry. I met someone who completes me. What I feel for her is more than two people who are comfortable together, like we are. I know I should have told you sooner. Face-to-face. But I really was going to marry you. Until I woke up this morning and just ... couldn't. Forgive me. I hope you find the love and excitement I have.*

Chloe's stomach twisted in a combination of hurt and embarrassment. Of all the cowardly actions ... that's what she got for choosing a man with a weak handshake who couldn't look her brothers in the eye. As they'd told her, over and over again, they hadn't thought Owen was good enough for her. But had she listened? Oh, no. She'd made her safe choice, and she'd intended to stick with her decision.

Had she loved Owen? Looking into her heart, she was forced to shake her head. No. She'd cared for him, that much was true. But love, like her brother and his best friend, Jordan, had found with each other? No, Chloe couldn't say she'd experienced that all-encompassing emotion.

In truth, love scared her, because her mom had loved her father so much she'd stayed in an extremely miserable marriage with a serial cheater and had lost out on the opportunity to embrace who she was and be happy. Maybe that was why Chloe was angry at Owen for how he'd handled things but not devastated over losing him.

Dammit. She lifted the bottle and took another long drink. She should have looked inward and called things off first, but who was she kidding? She never would have done it. Chloe was the good girl who always did the right thing, made the risk-free choices, and behaved as expected of her. Canceling the wedding wasn't something Chloe Kingston would ever have done.

A knock sounded loudly on the door, startling her. "Chloe? I'm coming in," her brother Linc called out.

She'd been alone in this room long enough, and she'd come to a decision, at least for tonight. It was time she told her family what she had planned.

"Okay!" she called out just as the door opened and Linc stepped inside, looking handsome in his black tuxedo. His gaze immediately zeroed in on the nearly empty champagne bottle in her hand.

"Not a word," she threatened him, waving the bottle in front of her. "I deserve this."

He nodded, his expression somber. "You do."

She lifted the bottle to her lips only to find it empty. Oh, well. There was more where this had come from. At least the bubbly liquid was beginning to do its trick, going to her head and lifting her mood.

Linc looked relieved and she chose not to enlighten him that, by the time the night was over, champagne would be the lightest drink she consumed.

"I'm sorry, Chloe. Owen's a bastard."

"Yes, he is. He should have told me sooner, and he should have done it in person. But he didn't and I have to handle the cards I've been dealt.

Linc nodded. "I'll go out and tell everyone to go home."

"No. Well, you can tell some of the guests to go home."

She pushed herself up from her chair and ignored the light spinning in her head. She hadn't had much to eat today, but there were appetizers galore almost ready to be served. At least that had been the post-ceremony agenda, followed by a three-course meal.

"What are you talking about?" Clearly concerned, Linc walked over and put a hand on her shoulder. "Mom wants you to come home with her. She and Aurora want to be there for you."

She thought about spending her wedding night in her mother's mansion-like house, her mom wringing her hands and trying not to cry for all Chloe had endured. "No. I want you to take Mom home. Take everyone in the family home." She stepped aside and his hand fell to his side.

Linc narrowed his gaze. "What about you?"

Her brother wasn't stupid and he knew her well. No doubt he saw the wheels in her mind spinning.

"You sublet your apartment and moved out. The

boxes are in storage because you were supposed to live with Owen after your honeymoon." He winced at the mention of more plans that wouldn't be happening.

Plans she had no intention of thinking about yet.

Chloe drew a deep breath. "I have the honeymoon suite booked in the hotel tonight. I'll stay here. *After* my friends and I take advantage of the party that's already paid for. I'll just call it my non-wedding party." She let out a champagne-induced laugh and spun around, grabbing for the counter before she fell over.

"Chloe," Linc said in his stern, big-brother voice.

Ignoring him, she sat down, hiked up her gown, and unhooked the straps on her too-high-heeled, glittering sandals. "I can't dance in these," she said, kicking them across the room.

Her brother, who always had an answer and a solution, appeared concerned and at a loss. Before Chloe could reassure him, he strode to the door, pulled it open, and yelled for his fiancée. "Jordan! Get in here!"

"Reinforcements won't help," Chloe warned him, letting out another laugh, this one more of a giggle. Apparently she'd had more to drink than she'd realized, and she'd always been a lightweight.

Jordan, a gorgeous woman with jet-black hair, wearing an exquisite emerald-green gown, which Chloe knew had had to be let out to accommodate her early-pregnancy belly, rushed inside. "Is everything okay?"

"Chloe thinks she's going to party with her friends tonight. She wants her family to leave. Tell her she needs to go home with Mom and let us all take care of her," Linc ordered.

His frown would scare off most people, but Chloe had grown up with him. He'd do his best to exert his command, but she'd made up her mind. And he'd never been able to intimidate Jordan, who glanced at Chloe.

A silent understanding passed between them, woman to woman.

Jordan had grown up the daughter of the Kingston family's housekeeper, yet she and Linc had been best friends for years, and she'd been his personal assistant since he'd joined Kingston Enterprises after earning his MBA. Of everyone, Jordan knew how to handle him best. She always had.

And Jordan also understood the need to make her own choices. Chloe had faith her soon-to-be sister-in-law would support her.

"Linc," Jordan said, walking up to him and wrapping an arm around his waist. "I think Chloe knows what she needs. You can't just order her around and expect her to listen."

He blinked in shock. "You think her getting drunk is the answer to what happened here?" he asked.

"I think," Jordan said slowly, "it couldn't hurt. Let

her do what she wants, and you can step in and play big brother tomorrow." She ran her hand over Linc's back. "I know you want to make it all better, but you can't. Not right now."

Chloe shot Jordan a grateful glance. "I owe you," she mouthed to her.

Chloe wished Jordan had taken her up on her offer to be a bridesmaid after she'd gotten engaged to Linc. But Jordan had issues with feeling like an outsider thanks to their very different backgrounds, and she felt she'd be coming in late and hadn't wanted to rock the boat. Chloe intended to make Jordan feel more like family than the closest family member. She still would do that after she celebrated her un-wedding.

"I don't like this," Linc muttered.

"You don't have to." Jordan tugged on his hand. "Let's go talk to the family." She glanced at Chloe. "Who do you want me to send in to be with you?"

Chloe forced a smile. "Send my bridesmaids in, please. And tell anyone who isn't family that wants to stay and party to stick around." She would enjoy tonight if it killed her.

"Chloe, why don't you let us stay, too?" Linc asked, attempting to handle things one last time.

"Because you'd all kill my fun. You'd sit around with concerned looks, waiting for me to fall apart. And I'd be worried about all of you, and that would defeat the purpose of a party." The explanation made sense to her.

"Linc, come." Jordan tugged at his hand, and soon she'd led him out of the room.

But not before he stopped, walked over to Chloe, and pulled her into a brotherly hug. "You deserve the very best, and I promise you the right person is out there. I love you, Chlo."

She tightened her arms around him, accepting the love she'd never gotten from her father. "I love you, too. Just let me have this night. Tomorrow is soon enough to face things."

Linc groaned. "Okay, Scarlett O'Hara. But we will talk then."

Of that, Chloe had no doubt.

In the morning, Linc would do his best to take over, and she'd just have to deal with him then. God, she adored her family. Her love life might suck, but she had a support system not many people could claim. The problem was, come tomorrow, she'd be smothered in worry by well-meaning relatives.

But tonight was for her.

After watching Linc and Jordan walk out, Chloe rose and dug for the ballet flats she'd planned to wear once her feet began to hurt. She slipped them on so she could dance. After all, they'd paid for a high-priced DJ, and she intended to enjoy every moment until she crashed. There might come a time when she cried, but she refused to think about her pain.

Just then, her friends piled into the room, and she braced herself to explain her plans for the evening one more time.

Then they'd have fun.

"HAPPY BIRTHDAY TO you. Happy birthday to you. Happy birthday, dear Dad, happy birthday to you." Beckett Daniels's family finished singing to their father and followed the lyrics with a round of applause.

"Make a wish, Kurt," Audrey, Beck's mom, said to her husband.

He looked around at his wife, Beck, and his other two sons, Drew and Tripp, and smiled, the gratitude in his expression obvious. Then he paused and blew out the candles.

Beck wondered, as he did every year, if his father wished for everyone sitting at this table's health and well-being. God knows that was Beck's annual birthday prayer. They'd all learned years ago how fragile life could be after losing Tripp's twin, Whitney, when they were teens.

The server reached over and lifted the cake. "We'll slice it and be right back. I'll take your coffee orders then," he said and walked away.

"I don't know about you but that cake looked delicious," his mother said. "And that frosting? Mmm. I can't wait."

Tripp, a pediatrician, grinned. "I'll take a big chunk, myself."

Andrew glanced at their father. "You look like you could use a slice, Dad. Have you lost weight?"

Beck shifted his gaze back to his father, noting the more drawn look in his lower face. "Now that Drew's mentioned it, you do look thinner."

His father waved a hand through the air. "I'm fine, boys. Don't worry about me."

Beck always worried. But tonight they were at his father's favorite steak restaurant. There might have been a time the Daniels family couldn't afford a restaurant this fancy or expensive, and Beck and his brothers had put themselves through school on loans, but they'd always had love. And now Beck, Tripp, or Drew could more than cover the cost of taking their parents out for an extravagant dinner.

His father looked up, his eyes widening. "And there's our dessert."

Beck tried to get his mother's attention to see if she'd give him an inkling about his dad's health, but she was busy digging into the cake the server had placed in front of her first. He held back a groan, telling himself he shouldn't jump to conclusions. It wasn't like he spent all his time thinking about his sister, but she was always there, ready to pop into his mind and remind him how quickly things could change. How fast life could turn to loss.

"Beck? I asked if you'd like a piece?" his mom asked.

He nodded, knowing it would make her happy. "Hit me up," he said. "And make it a big slice." Pushing sad thoughts out of his head, he focused on enjoying the here and now. Something he was still learning how to do, many, many years later. Losing a sibling to leukemia had been harsh and difficult, and they all still suffered the aftereffects all this time later.

"Hey, when we finish eating, who wants to head to the bar downstairs and have a drink?" Drew, the lawyer in the family, asked.

"I'm in," Tripp said, shoveling the cake in his mouth as he spoke.

Laughing, Beck lifted a piece onto his fork. "I'll join you," he said, then took the cake into this mouth. The chocolate melted and he damn near moaned out loud. "This is amazing," he said, going in for another bite.

"Mom? Dad?" Tripp turned their way. "Want to come?"

"Oh, no. You boys stay out and have some fun. We're just going to go home like the old people we are." She grinned and they all rolled their eyes.

His mom had married his father after she'd graduated college. Then she'd gotten pregnant with Drew at the age of twenty-three. Now fifty-eight, she looked a lot younger than her years. Nobody would call either of his parents *old*. But if they wanted to go home, everyone understood.

A little while later, with the check taken care of and goodbyes said to their parents, Beck, Tripp, and Drew made their way out of the restaurant and headed toward the main lobby bar.

A nighttime hotspot, the lobby was crowded, people lining up past the entrance and mingling in the main room and around the fountain in the center.

"I guess we're not getting near the drinks any time soon," Drew muttered.

"Doesn't seem like it." Tripp stopped walking so they could talk and regroup.

"Do you want to go somewhere else? Or we could head back to my apartment and have a few drinks there." Beck didn't care as long as he spent time with his siblings.

"Your place sounds good. I'm not looking to pick anyone up tonight," Drew said.

"I'll get us an Uber." Tripp pulled out his cell.

They began to head toward the side entrance where it was quieter and they could more easily locate their ride share when a burst of feminine laughter caught Beck's attention.

He glanced up in time to see a bride walking across the lobby, surrounded by three other women in matching dresses.

"Gives a whole other meaning to women going to the ladies' room together," Beck said to his brothers.

Tripp laughed only to be tag teamed by two of the bridesmaids.

"Ooh, you're cute," a pretty brunette said.

"I saw him first, Wendy. Go find your own guy." The proprietary woman grabbed Tripp's elbow and hung on tight.

Beck's sibling raised his eyebrows but didn't attempt to disengage his new appendage.

"I'll take this one then." The woman with auburn hair latched on to Drew.

Beck didn't know whether to be insulted or relieved that none of the women had chosen him.

"I know you!" The bride, who had obviously gotten waylaid because she just joined them now, tripped and fell against Beck's chest.

He braced his hands on her bare forearms, steadying her as he helped her stand up straight. When she didn't wobble, he released her and met her gaze. Long blond hair fell in waves around her exquisite face, and blue eyes with a darker rim around the edges stared back at him, reminding him of someone he knew.

"Beckett Daniels, right?" she asked.

"Yes." There was a familiarity to her features. He knew her, he just couldn't place her. "And you're…"

"Chloe Kingston. Linc's sister." She treated him to a megawatt smile that had the power to knock him on his ass.

Son. Of. A. Bitch. Linc, his one-time best friend. Now a man he barely spoke to.

"You and my brother are business competitors," she said and let out a little hiccup. Clearly she was as drunk as her bridesmaids.

"That would be putting it mildly." But he wasn't about to elaborate on his relationship with her brother. If Linc hadn't seen fit to tell her the sordid details, he wasn't going to go there, either. It was a time in his life he'd much rather forget.

Looking at Chloe, her flushed cheeks, in her inebriated state, he assumed the ceremony had already taken place. "So you kept your maiden name?" he asked. Because she hadn't introduced herself as Chloe Kingston Something-or-Other.

"Oh, no. No, no, no." She waved her hand through the air, her long nails a pale white color. "I'm not married." A deeper flush rose to her face. "I was left at the altar."

Beck blinked, then stared at her, stunned. "What

kind of asshole would stand up a gorgeous woman like you?" Despite her relation to his sworn enemy, Beck couldn't deny the fact that the girl he'd met in college was all grown up and one hell of a knockout.

"You're sweet." She sniffed and he was afraid he'd triggered a crying jag, but she forced a smile instead. "He found someone who *completes him*," she said, using quotation marks with her fingers. "And he hopes I *find the love and excitement he has*." She finished with more finger quotes.

She sniffed again. "But the bastard did it by text. And I'm celebrating because everything is paid for, and I think just maybe he did me a favor. Even if I sometimes want to cry." She fluttered her thick black lashes, and Beck was afraid she'd do just that.

He didn't know what to make of Chloe or what to do with her. On the one hand, he wanted to beat the crap out of the man who'd hurt her. On the other, he needed to remember she was Linc's sister and he ought to stay far away.

"Anyway." Chloe interrupted his train of thought, which was going in a direction he didn't like but which still held some appeal. "I figured why let everything go to waste? So we're partying! Come with me!" she said, tugging on his sleeve.

He glanced at his brothers, who were preoccupied with her bridesmaids, and rolled his eyes. No matter what they decided to do, he was not going in there and dealing with her brother.

"I don't think that's a good idea."

Her wide smile dimmed. "Why not? You want to dump me, too?" Her pout was too fucking adorable, and her words hit him in the gut.

"No, I don't want to dump a beautiful … umm … bride like you. But Linc and I aren't on the best of terms."

"Oh!" Her smile returned. "Well, that's no problem. Linc's not here. I made my family go home. I didn't want to see their sad, worried faces at my non-wedding party." She flung her arm, gesturing toward the double doors on the far side of the lobby.

"Your brother left you drunk after being … well, he just left?" Beck stopped himself before he reminded her she'd been dumped.

Still, he was shocked. She had three brothers. If she were *his* sister, no way would Beck have abandoned her on a night like this. Then again, *his* sister wouldn't have the opportunity to fall in love or get married, though it had been on the bucket list she'd made near the end. A list of experiences she wished she could have and ones she wanted Beck to enjoy in her place.

"Come dance with me." Chloe slipped her soft hand into his, raised his arm, and twirled around until dizziness had her crashing into him once more.

He found himself wrapping an arm around her waist and hauling her sweet curves against him. Inhaling, he took in her delectable, warm scent and wanted to bury his face in her neck and nibble on her fragrant skin. His cock jerked in agreement.

"What do you say? Are we going to party with the ladies?" Tripp asked, glancing at Drew, his arm around the brunette, before looking back at Beck.

His brothers, like Beck, dated without thinking about settling down. They probably saw these women as easy pickings.

Beck felt Chloe's body, soft and warm against his. He glanced down and her gorgeous eyes stared back at him, those lips puckered up like she was waiting for a kiss.

Jesus. How could he send her off to continue getting wasted on her own? At least that's the excuse he gave himself when he nodded at his brother and said, "Why not? Let's go party."

"Yay!" Chloe clapped her hands, her pleasure obvious. Then she grasped his hand and led him toward the ballroom, his brothers and their women following.

The room had been decked out for a gala. Between the flowers, the décor, the gold chairs, and the centerpieces, no money had been spared. His heart hurt for the drunk would-have-been bride. He might despise her brother, but Beck wouldn't blame his sister for Linc's actions or wish bad things on other people in their family.

"Let's dance," she said and, without waiting for him, sashayed onto the makeshift dance floor.

Before deciding whether or not to join her, he watched as she began to sway to the music, her body coming alive to the beat. A veritable princess in her ballroom gown. What kind of asshole would dump this woman? From being in the real estate business, he was aware of her job as Kingston Enterprises' lead decorator. She furnished any building purchased or leased out by Kingston Enterprises, and though their aesthetic was more staid than what Beck and his company preferred, Chloe was clearly beautiful as well as talented.

And the Kingston family, like Beck himself, was often the subject of tabloid gossip about the rich and famous. Which meant the devastation she was trying so hard to hide would soon be public knowledge. There was no avoiding that.

Maybe he should help her enjoy the night before she had to face her future. He stepped toward the dance floor just as another man joined her and pulled her to him, obviously grinding against her. She braced her hands on his shoulders in a clear attempt to push him away.

Beck rushed forward and shoved at the guy's shoulder, breaking his hold on Chloe.

"What the fuck?" the man asked, his gaze going

from the woman in the wedding gown to Beck. "She invited me. She came into the bar earlier and said she wants to party. I was just showing her a good time."

Beck frowned, realizing Chloe's *non-wedding* could get out of hand. "Well, she changed her mind, and she isn't interested in what you're offering. Get lost or I'll have you thrown out."

"I don't need this shit." The guy glared at Chloe before he turned and strode out.

One crisis averted, Beck thought.

Chloe grasped his arm and sighed. "Thank you. You're my hero!" She lifted her arms and flung herself against him, giving him a nose full of her fruity-smelling hair. Once again her soft curves crushed his chest, tempting him, and his dick reacted.

Down, boy, he thought, because Chloe was in no frame of mind to fall into bed with a virtual stranger. It would be no better than taking advantage of her, and Beck would never stoop so low. Not to mention, he'd had a sister and he'd kick the ass of anyone who'd exploited her.

He looked overhead and saw his brothers having fun with the bridesmaids. They seemed fine and could take care of themselves. Catching Tripp's gaze, he mouthed he was leaving and his brother nodded.

Beck braced his hands on Chloe's waist and eased her away from him, looking into her glassy eyes. Yep, time to get this bride to bed.

"Come on, princess," he said because that's what she resembled. A fairy-tale princess. "Time to go. I'll take you home."

Her lower lip trembled, the first sign of outward fragility and hurt she'd shown since targeting him in the lobby. "I don't have a home. All my things are in boxes. I was going to move them into Owen's house after the wedding."

"Owen the douchebag, huh? Okay, then how about your mom's?" Her father had passed away a few months ago from a heart attack. While most people in the industry had shown up for the funeral, Beck had passed.

"Owen the douchebag." She giggled at his description. "And no, I'm not going to my mother's with my tail between my legs like a little girl." She shook her head back and forth. "Nope. Not happening."

He groaned. "One of your brothers, then?" And he'd better not have to show up with her on Linc's doorstep.

She shook her head again, her expression adamant. "Either they'll say I told you so or they'll hover."

Obviously neither option appealed to her.

"Don't worry though. I have a plan," she said, surprising him. "We'd rented the honeymoon suite for the night. I'll just crash there."

She started to walk away, but if this were a sobriety

test, she'd fail in a heartbeat. She wobbled her first few steps, tripped, and he darted forward, making a split-second decision before she took a header onto the floor. Lifting her, he adjusted her until she was more secure. Her delicate arms wrapped around him, and she buried her face in the crook of his neck and shoulder.

"I'm tired." Her lips moved against his skin, her breath warm against his flesh.

At the arousing sensation, his entire body shook with need. "Fuck," he muttered as he walked, ignoring the stares as he carried her out of the ballroom.

"Can we?" she asked without lifting her head from his shoulder.

He stifled a groan. "No. You're going to go upstairs to pass out cold." Another man, the man he wished he could be, would take advantage of her just to show Linc Kingston what betrayal felt like.

But Beck had been raised right.

He stopped at the front desk and roused Chloe long enough for her to ask for her room key. Obviously they already knew her, and the bridal dress pretty much said it all. The man behind the counter handed over the key. And Beck made his way upstairs with the passed-out-again bride in his arms.

Read **Just One Scandal**.

Want even more Carly books?

CARLY'S BOOKLIST by Series – visit:
https://www.carlyphillips.com/CPBooklist

Sign up for Carly's Newsletter:
https://www.carlyphillips.com/CPNewsletter

Join Carly's Corner on Facebook:
https://www.carlyphillips.com/CarlysCorner

Carly on Facebook:
https://www.carlyphillips.com/CPFanpage

Carly on Instagram:
https://www.carlyphillips.com/CPInstagram

Carly's Booklist

The Dare Series

Dare to Love Series
Book 1: Dare to Love (Ian & Riley)
Book 2: Dare to Desire (Alex & Madison)
Book 3: Dare to Touch (Dylan & Olivia)
Book 4: Dare to Hold (Scott & Meg)
Book 5: Dare to Rock (Avery & Grey)
Book 6: Dare to Take (Tyler & Ella)
A Very Dare Christmas – Short Story (Ian & Riley)

** Sienna Dare gets together with Ethan Knight in **The Knight Brothers** (Dare Me Tonight).*

** Jason Dare gets together with Faith in the **Sexy Series** (More Than Sexy).*

Dare NY Series (NY Dare Cousins)
Book 1: Dare to Surrender (Gabe & Isabelle)
Book 2: Dare to Submit (Decklan & Amanda)
Book 3: Dare to Seduce (Max & Lucy)

The Knight Brothers
Book 1: Take Me Again (Sebastian & Ashley)
Book 2: Take Me Down (Parker & Emily)
Book 3: Dare Me Tonight (Ethan Knight & Sienna Dare)
Novella: Take The Bride (Sierra & Ryder)
Take Me Now – Short Story (Harper & Matt)

The Sexy Series
Book 1: More Than Sexy (Jason Dare & Faith)

Book 2: Twice As Sexy (Tanner & Scarlett)
Book 3: Better Than Sexy (Landon & Vivienne)
Novella: Sexy Love (Shane & Amber)

Dare Nation
Book 1: Dare to Resist (Austin & Quinn)
Book 2: Dare to Tempt (Damon & Evie)
Book 3: Dare to Play (Jaxon & Macy)
Book 4: Dare to Stay (Brandon & Willow)
Novella: Dare to Tease (Hudson & Brianne)

* Paul Dare's sperm donor kids

Kingston Family
Book 1: Just One Night (Linc Kingston & Jordan Greene)
Book 2: Just One Scandal (Chloe Kingston & Beck Daniels)
Book 3: Just One Chance (Xander Kingston & Sasha Keaton)
Book 4: Just One Spark (Dash Kingston & Cassidy Forrester)
Book 5: Just One Wish (Axel Forrester)
Book 6: Just One Dare (Aurora Kingston & Nick Dare)
Book 7: Just One Kiss
Book 8: Just One Taste

For the most recent Carly books, visit CARLY'S BOOKLIST page
www.carlyphillips.com/CPBooklist

Other Indie Series

Billionaire Bad Boys

Book 1: Going Down Easy

Book 2: Going Down Hard

Book 3: Going Down Fast

Book 4: Going In Deep

Going Down Again – Short Story

Hot Heroes Series

Book 1: Touch You Now

Book 2: Hold You Now

Book 3: Need You Now

Book 4: Want You Now

Bodyguard Bad Boys

Book 1: Rock Me

Book 2: Tempt Me

Novella: His To Protect

For the most recent Carly books, visit CARLY'S
BOOKLIST page

www.carlyphillips.com/CPBooklist

Carly's Originally Traditionally Published Books

Serendipity Series
Book 1: Serendipity
Book 2: Destiny
Book 3: Karma

Serendipity's Finest Series
Book 1: Perfect Fling
Book 2: Perfect Fit
Book 3: Perfect Together

Serendipity Novellas
Book 1: Fated
Book 2: Perfect Stranger

The Chandler Brothers
Book 1: The Bachelor
Book 2: The Playboy
Book 3: The Heartbreaker

Hot Zone
Book 1: Hot Stuff
Book 2: Hot Number
Book 3: Hot Item
Book 4: Hot Property

Costas Sisters
Book 1: Under the Boardwalk
Book 2: Summer of Love

Lucky Series
Book 1: Lucky Charm
Book 2: Lucky Break
Book 3: Lucky Streak

Bachelor Blogs
Book 1: Kiss Me if You Can
Book 2: Love Me If You Dare

Ty and Hunter
Book 1: Cross My Heart
Book 2: Sealed with a Kiss

Carly Classics (Unexpected Love)
Book 1: The Right Choice
Book 2: Perfect Partners
Book 3: Unexpected Chances
Book 4: Suddenly Love
Book 5: Worthy of Love

Carly Classics (The Simply Series)
Book 1: Simply Sinful
Book 2: Simply Scandalous
Book 3: Simply Sensual
Book 4: Body Heat
Book 5: Simply Sexy

For the most recent Carly books, visit CARLY'S
BOOKLIST page
www.carlyphillips.com/CPBooklist

Carly's Still Traditionally Published Books

Stand-Alone Books

Brazen

Secret Fantasy

Seduce Me

The Seduction

More Than Words Volume 7 – Compassion Can't Wait

Naughty Under the Mistletoe

Grey's Anatomy 101 Essay

Grey's Anatomy 101 Essay

For the most recent Carly books, visit CARLY'S BOOKLIST page

www.carlyphillips.com/CPBooklist

About the Author

NY Times, Wall Street Journal, and USA Today Bestseller, Carly Phillips is the queen of Alpha Heroes, at least according to The Harlequin Junkie Reviewer. Carly married her college sweetheart and lives in Purchase, NY along with her crazy dogs who are featured on her Facebook and Instagram pages. The author of over 75 romance novels, she has raised two incredible daughters and is now an empty nester. Carly's book, The Bachelor, was chosen by Kelly Ripa as her first romance club pick. Carly loves social media and interacting with her readers. Want to keep up with Carly? Sign up for her newsletter and receive TWO FREE books at www.carlyphillips.com.

Made in United States
Troutdale, OR
12/29/2023

16548605R00176